Uncle Montague's Tales of Terror

Also *by* Chris Priestley

Tales of Terror from the Black Ship
Tales of Terror from the Tunnel's Mouth

Coming soon

The Dead of Winter

UNCLE
MONTAGUE'S
TALES
OF
TERROR

CHRIS PRIESTLEY

ILLUSTRATED BY DAVID ROBERTS

BLOOMSBURY

LONDON BERLIN NEW YORK

Bloomsbury Publishing, London, Berlin and New York

First published in Great Britain in October 2007 by Bloomsbury Publishing Plc
36 Soho Square, London, W1D 3QY

This edition first published in 2010

A CIP catalogue record of this book is available from the British Library

ISBN 978 1 4088 1370 6

FSC
Mixed Sources
Product group from well-managed
forests and other controlled sources

Cert no. SGS - COC - 2061
www.fsc.org
© 1996 Forest Stewardship Council

Typeset by Dorchester Typesetting Group Ltd
Printed in Great Britain by Clays Ltd, St Ives plc, Bungay, Suffolk

1 3 5 7 9 10 8 6 4 2

www.bloomsbury.com
www.TalesofTerror.co.uk

For Sally

CONTENTS

THROUGH
THE
WOODS

The way to Uncle Montague's house lay through a small wood. The path coiled between the trees like a snake hiding in a thicket, and though the path was not long and the wood not at all large, that part of the journey always seemed to take far longer than I would ever have thought it could.

It had become a habit of mine to visit my uncle during the school holidays. I was an only child and my parents were not comfortable around children. My father tried his best, putting his hand on my shoulder and pointing various things out to me, but when he had run out of things to point at, he was overcome with a kind of sullen melancholy and left the house to go shooting alone for hours. My mother was of a nervous disposition and seemed unable to relax in my company, leaping to her feet with a small cry whenever I moved, cleaning and polishing everything I touched or sat upon.

'He's an odd fish,' said my father one day at breakfast.

'Who is?' said my mother.

'Uncle Montague,' he replied.

'Yes,' she agreed. 'Very odd. What do you and he do all afternoon when you visit him, Edgar?'

'He tells me stories,' I said.

'Good Lord,' said my father. 'Stories, eh? I heard a story once.'

'Yes, Father?' I said expectantly. My father frowned and looked at his plate.

'No,' he said. 'It's gone.'

'Never mind, darling,' said my mother. 'I'm sure it was marvellous.'

'Oh, it was,' he said. 'It really was.' He chuckled to himself. 'Marvellous, yes.'

Uncle Montague lived in a house nearby. He was not strictly speaking my uncle, rather some kind of great-uncle, but as an argument had broken out between my parents about exactly how many 'greats' there should be, in the end I thought it best to simply call him 'Uncle'.

I have no recollection of ever visiting him when the trees of the wood between our houses were in leaf. All my memories of walking through that wood are when it was cold with frost or snow and the only leaves I ever saw were dead and rotting on the ground.

At the far side of the wood there was a kissing gate: one of the kind that lets only one person through at a time while ensuring that the gate cannot be left open and allow sheep to escape. I cannot think why the wood or the paddock it bordered had such a gate, for I never did see any creatures whatever in that field or anywhere at all on my uncle's property. Well, none that you could call livestock at any rate.

I never liked the kissing gate. It had a devilishly strong spring and my uncle did not have it oiled as often as he might. In any event, I never once passed through without feeling the strangest horror of being trapped. In the odd state of panic that came over me, I foolishly imagined that something was coming at me behind my back.

Of course, in no time at all, I managed to pull back the creaking gate and squeeze through, and each time would turn with relief to see the wood unchanged beyond the small stone wall I had just passed through. Even so, in my childish way, I would turn again as I set out across the paddock, hoping (or rather perhaps *dreading*) to catch sight of someone – or something. But I never did.

That said, I did sometimes have company on my walk. The children from the village would occasionally skulk about. I had nothing to do with them, nor they with me. I was away at school. I do not wish to sound a snob, but we came from different worlds.

I would sometimes see them among the trees, as I did this particular day. They did not come near and never said a word. They stood silently among the shadows. Their intention was clearly to intimidate me, and in that they were quite successful, but I did my best not to appear ruffled. I made a show of ignoring them and continued on my way.

The paddock was overgrown with long ragged grass and the dry brown seed heads of thistles and teasels and cow parsley. As I walked across the track of trampled grass towards the garden gate, I could see and hear the scampering movement of what I took to be rabbits or pheasants, rustling in the undergrowth.

I always paused at the gate to look at the house, which stood on its own little hillock as many churches do, and indeed there was something of the graveyard in its walled garden and something of the church in its arched Gothic windows and its spikes and ornaments. The garden gate was as much in need of oil as the kissing gate and the latch so heavy that it took all my boyish strength to lift it, the metal so cold and damp it chilled my fingers to the bone.

When I turned to shut the gate again, I would always look back and marvel at how my parents' house was now entirely hidden by the wood, and at how, in the particular stillness of that place, it seemed that there was no other living soul for miles about.

The path now led across the lawn to my uncle's door, past a strange gathering of topiary bushes. No doubt these massive yews had once been artfully clipped into the usual array of cones and birds, but for some years they had been growing wild. These feral bushes now stood malevolently about the house, inviting the imagination to see in their deformed shapes the hint of teeth, the suggestion of a leathery wing, the illusion of a claw or an eye.

I knew, of course, that they were only bushes, but

nevertheless I am embarrassed to say that I always found myself hurrying along the path that led between them, and was never tempted to look over my shoulder as I rapped the great hoop of the door knocker to announce my presence to my uncle – a hoop, I should say, which hung from the mouth of a most peculiar creature: the face, formed of dull unpolished brass, seemed to hover unnervingly betwixt lion and man.

After what always seemed an extraordinary length of time, and just as I was about to lift the door knocker again, the door would open and Uncle Montague would be standing there, as always, holding a candle and smiling at me, beckoning me to enter.

'Don't stand there in the cold, Edgar,' he said. 'Come in, lad. Come in.'

I entered eagerly enough, but to tell the truth there was little difference in temperature between the garden and my uncle's hallway, and if there *was* a difference I would say it was in the garden's favour, for I have never been so cold *inside* a building as I was inside my uncle's house. I swear I once saw frost sparkling on the banisters of the stairs.

My uncle set off along the stone-flagged hall and I set off in pursuit, following the flickering candlelight as keenly as a moth. It was part of my uncle's many eccentricities that, though he clearly did not want for money, he never had any truck with electric light – nor gaslight for that matter – and lit the house by candle wax alone, and that sparingly. Following behind him, therefore, towards his study was always a disconcerting business, for in spite of being in the safety of my uncle's house, I did not feel comfortable to be left in the dark there and hurried my steps to keep in contact with both him and the light.

As my uncle walked through the draughty house the candlelight no doubt added to my jitters: its fluttering passage created all kinds of grotesque shadows on the wall, which danced and leaped about, giving the unnerving impression of gaining a life of their own and scuttling away to hide under pieces of furniture or scurry up walls to skulk in ceiling corners.

After more walking than seemed possible from the size of the house as it appeared from outside, we arrived at my uncle's study: a large room lined with shelves holding books and curios from the old man's travels. The walls were encrusted with prints and paintings, and heavy curtains smothered the leaded windows. No matter that it was still afternoon – the study was as sunless as a cave.

The floor was covered in a rich Persian carpet and the base colour of that carpet was a deep red, as were the paintwork of the walls and the damask fabric of the curtains. A large fire burned in the grate and made the colour glow, throbbing rhythmically at the movement of the flames, as if this room were the beating heart of the house.

Certainly it was the only part of the house I ever saw that I could describe as comfortable, though I should say at this point that despite having been to my uncle's house many times this was in fact the *only* room I had ever been in (save for the lavatory).

This may seem odd, but it did not occur to me as such at the time. My meetings with Uncle Montague were less of a family get-together and more in the way of a business appointment. Uncle and I were very fond of one another in our way, but we both knew what had brought me: hunger – hunger for stories.

'Sit yourself down, young fellow,' he said (as he always did). 'I'll ring and see if Franz will consent to bring us some tea and cakes.'

Uncle pulled on the long sash by the fireplace and as usual I strained to hear a bell sound far away in the house. Footsteps gradually became audible and grew in volume as they slowly progressed towards the study door. They stopped outside and there followed a long pause and then three alarmingly loud knocks.

The door handle turned, rattling as it did so, and the door opened. From where I sat the door blocked my view and all I could see was my uncle standing by the open door, whispering our request before the door slowly closed once more and the footsteps faded away into the distance, oddly mingling with their own echoes to produce a strange scampering sound.

I should like to have told you something of Franz's appearance, as I am sure you will be wondering if he was tall or fat or fair-haired, but I am afraid that never on any of my visits did I so much as catch the merest glimpse of Franz.

By the time my uncle and I had exchanged some pleasantries and he had enquired as to the current state of my schooling, there were three more sonorous knocks at the door, and Uncle, getting up to answer it once again, returned with a tray, on which there was a large tea pot, cups and saucers, and a plate of cakes and biscuits. There was no milk jug because Uncle and I both took our tea black. There was a bowl of sugar lumps and, though I never saw him actually take one, my uncle must have had a considerable sweet tooth, for they were always entirely gone by the time I left, and I never took sugar at all, even as a small boy.

We sat either side of the fire, my uncle and I, with the tray on a small table between us, my uncle with his elbows on the arms of his chair and his fingertips together. When he leaned back, his face disappeared into shadow entirely.

'Your journey here was uneventful, I trust?' he asked.

'Yes, Uncle,' I said.

'You saw . . . nothing – in the woods?'

Uncle Montague often asked this question, and my reply was always the same.

'No, Uncle,' I said, not seeing the need to mention the village children, as I could not imagine they would be of interest to a man like my uncle. 'I did not see anything in the woods.'

My uncle smiled strangely and nodded, taking a sip of tea. He sighed wistfully.

'There is nothing quite like a wood at night, eh, Edgar?' he said.

'No,' I replied, trying to sound as though I might have some knowledge of nocturnal woodland.

'And where should mankind be without trees?'

he continued. 'Timber is the very engine of civilisation, Edgar: from the plough to paper, from the wheel to the house, from tool handles to sailing ships. Man would have been nothing without trees, lad.' He went to put another log on the hearth and the flames seemed to almost leap out and wrest it from his grip. 'After all, what could symbolise man's separation from the animal world more than fire – fire's warmth and fire's light?' We both looked into the fire, mesmerised for a while by its dancing flames.

'The Norse people believed that the world was suspended in the branches of a great ash tree. Did you know that, Edgar?'

'No, Uncle.'

'Yes,' he said. 'The people of the northern forests have always had a special relationship with the tree. After all, those ancient wild woods were their storehouse of building materials and fuel and food . . . But they were also dark and mysterious, filled with bears and robbers and who knows what else . . .'

'Do you mean . . . witches, Uncle?'

His eyes twinkled. 'Witches, warlocks, wizards, wood sprites, werewolves –'

'Werewolves?' I said with a little gulp.

'Perhaps.' Uncle Montague gave a little shrug.

'The point is they respected the forest and they respected trees – feared them – worshipped them.'

'How did they worship them, Uncle?' I said, taking a biscuit and noticing that the sugar was already gone.

'In many ways, I am sure,' he said. 'The Roman historians tell us of sacred groves, of oak trees splashed with blood –'

'Blood?' I said, spluttering a little on my biscuit.

'Yes,' said Uncle Montague. 'They tell of sacrifice – sometimes human. The Celts were partial to taking the heads of their enemies as trophies in battle. To them, the hanging of the heads on an oak was probably as festive as the hanging of baubles on a Christmas tree is to your dear mother.'

I raised a doubtful eyebrow on both counts and Uncle smiled.

'But why worship a tree?' I said.

'I can think of many things less deserving of worship,' he replied. 'Look at how long some trees have been alive. Think of what they have seen. Why, there are yew trees in churchyards that may be more than a thousand years old – older still than the ancient church nearby. Their roots are in one millennium and their branches in another. And who cannot stand in awe when they see a great oak or ash or elm standing alone like a mournful giant?'

He tapped his fingertips together and I saw his wolfish smile in the shadow. 'I know a story about just such a tree,' said my uncle. 'Would you like to hear it, Edgar?'

'Very much so.' After all, that was why I was there.

'It may be a little frightening for you.'

'I don't mind, Uncle,' I said with more courage than I felt, for I was like someone who, having been hauled to the highest point of a fairground ride, was beginning to have second thoughts.

'Very well,' said Uncle Montague, looking into the fire. 'Then I shall begin . . .'

The garden was enclosed on all sides by a high stone wall that was splashed and speckled with yellow, grey and cream-white lichen. To the east this wall housed tall gates of dark wood that opened on to a long gravel drive. To the west the wall had a smaller opening. Set between two fiercely spiked shrubs was a scratched and weathered, arched, bottle-green door with a heavy wrought-iron hoop to lift the latch that held it shut.

Beyond this door was a pasture of about two acres, bordered by the garden wall itself on one side, a hedge of hawthorn, hazel and dogwood on another, and a wooden post and rail fence on the other two. Almost in the centre of this pasture was an enormous and very ancient tree.

Joseph's father had proudly pointed the tree out to him as he took Joseph on a tour of their magnificent new house and grounds. Joseph's father was not given to great shows of emotion and seemed to save all his passion for his work, which Joseph did not fully understand, save that it was something to do with money and the making of money. But as he showed Joseph the tree his father seemed unusually sentimental.

He put his arm around Joseph, awkwardly but tenderly, and said, 'Do you see that tree, son? The old elm? What a giant! Isn't it marvellous? It must be hundreds of years old. The things it must have seen, eh?'

Joseph had to admit that the ancient elm really was rather marvellous. Standing there in the centre of the pasture, it looked like an animal in a paddock, or rather like a zoo animal in its enclosure – penned, but not in any way tame.

'I've got something for you,' said his father. 'I hope you like it.'

He handed Joseph a small blue box which, when opened, revealed a shining gold pocket watch.

'Oh!' said Joseph. 'Is that really for me? Thank you, Father.'

'Go on,' he said with a smile. 'Put it on. But don't lose it for God's sake. It was damned expensive.'

With a little help from his father, Joseph threaded the watch chain through the button hole of his waistcoat and tucked the watch into the pocket, where it ticked satisfyingly next to his ribs.

Joseph's father went back to London the following day. He had rooms near the City and spent most of his time there, coming back to the house at weekends. Because Joseph was away himself, at school, this arrangement did not usually affect him. But though he rarely missed his parents while at school, he was embarrassed to find himself holding back tears as he waved his father goodbye at the end of the drive.

'Come on,' said his mother, understanding something of the sadness in her son's eyes. 'Let's take Jess for a walk.'

So Joseph, his mother and Jess, the family spaniel, set off through the garden gate and across the pasture. There was a stile at the bottom, leading on to a footpath across some common land and through a lovely wood of oaks and beech and sweet chestnut.

The grass in the pasture had yet to be cut. It was long and blond, hissing with crickets and spattered with blood red poppies. Towering up above it all was the mighty elm.

Jess ran a zigzag, sniffing path, as she so often did, but today the tree seemed to demand her special attention. Joseph noticed for the first time that there was a cave-like hollow at the base of the tree and it was this that particularly interested her.

The spaniel sniffed the air and approached the hole cautiously, peering in, her ears alternately cocked for any noise and then held back against her head. Joseph could hear her whimpering quietly, as though she were mumbling under her breath.

Joseph and his mother smiled as they watched Jess inching her way forward. Her ears suddenly cocked again and she tilted her head to one side. She seemed to have heard a noise inside. She took a step forward and leaned tentatively into the hole.

Suddenly she gave a strange strangled yelp that almost sounded like a human scream of panic. It was so startling in its oddness that Joseph and his mother both flinched. Jess jolted backwards from the tree and tore off across the pasture as if pursued by a demon.

When she got to the garden door she could not

get through because the door was heavy and opened outwards. She whined and howled and scrabbled at the door, scratching the wood and digging the earth beneath it in a frantic effort to escape. Joseph ran back calling her name. When he reached her and tried to calm her down, she turned, wild-eyed, and bit him.

Jess had never bitten Joseph, not even as a puppy, and he could see that she barely recognised him. She seemed to have no room in her mind for anything other than the overwhelming urge to escape. He opened the door for her and she bolted, skidding on the gravel of the drive as she sped through the gates and away down the road.

'It's all right, Joey,' said his mother. 'Don't worry. She'll come back.'

But she did not.

It had been a long time since Joseph had cried, but he cried for Jess. Playing with her was one of the things he most looked forward to when he came home from school for the holidays. His mother said they must not give up hope that she would turn up safe and sound. They placed adverts in the local newspaper offering a reward but heard nothing.

When Joseph's father returned from London a

week later he took his son for a walk in the pasture. He told him that Jess might not come back and, were that to be the case, then they would get another dog. But Joseph did not want another dog. He wanted Jess.

Joseph's father crouched down, looked into the hole at the tree's roots and reached into it with his hand.

'No!' said Joseph with more force than he had intended. His father retracted his hand immediately.

'What is it?' he said.

'There . . . there . . . might be rats or something,' said Joseph. In truth he did not know why it had panicked him so to see his father put his hand into the hole, but though his father chuckled and ruffled his hair, he did not return to the hole and asked Mr Farlow, the gardener, to put poison down it.

Joseph's father returned to London as he always did, and Joseph fidgeted about the house until his mother shooed him out. Eventually he found himself in the pasture again, standing in front of the tree.

The desire to climb the tree came suddenly, without any prior thought on the subject, but as soon as it did, the impulse was overwhelming.

As he was looking for a way to begin, he noticed something written on the tree. CLIMB NOT had been crudely gouged into the bark, though it must have been many years ago, for the tree had healed around the wound of the words so that they were ancient scars in its elephant hide.

This discovery, though interesting, did not detain Joseph for long. It clearly did not apply to him, as the writer and intended reader must be long dead.

But no sooner had Joseph grabbed the very first branch than a voice behind him made him jump.

'I wouldn't do that if I were you.' It was old Mr Farlow. 'Heed what's writ there.'

'What?' said Joseph.

'I know you read it, lad,' he said. 'I saw you. Heed it.'

'I'm not scared,' said Joseph. 'I've climbed lots of trees.'

'Not this one. You know what they say about elms, don't you, boy?' said the old man with an unpleasant smile. '"Elms hateth man and waiteth." So keep away!'

Joseph turned and stomped away back towards the house and sulked for several hours, refusing to give his mother any clue as to what was bothering him. That night he watched from his bedroom window as the crown of the elm tree shook like the mane of a giant lion, black against the indigo night, roaring in the wind. Joseph would show that old fool.

By asking his mother a succession of apparently innocent questions over breakfast the next day, Joseph discovered that Mr Farlow did not come to work on the gardens on Thursdays. That was two days away, and Joseph awaited the arrival of Mr Farlow's day off as keenly as if it had been both Christmas Day and his own birthday rolled into one. His excitement surprised him – frightened him even – but he seemed to have no choice but to give in to it.

On Thursday afternoon he dashed out of the house unnoticed, ran all the way to the elm and stood gasping for breath in its shadow. After gazing up into the branches above him, he set about climbing.

Joseph quickly discovered that the tree was going to be harder to climb than he had expected, but this only made the climbing of it more of an adventure. Even when he missed his footing and slipped, scraping his knee on the grizzled bark and almost falling, he felt the pain to be a sign of his commitment to the climb.

He reached a branch about thirty feet from the ground and could find no way of continuing. He tried to reach a branch above him, but looking down he lost his nerve and could go no further. He took out his new watch. It was getting late.

Reluctantly Joseph climbed down, trying to retrace his route, vowing to return the following Thursday to continue the climb. He jumped the last few feet, landing with a soft thud on the ground.

As he landed he had the strangest impression that there was a muffled echo of his landing, that something beneath the earth had flinched or flexed. The hole at the tree's base seemed darker and more impenetrable than ever. He took two tentative steps forward, leaning to peer in, but found that he could not make himself go closer.

He walked back across the pasture with a carefree gait that was completely feigned. In reality he was resisting an impulse to run. He was almost at the door in the wall, when he turned round quickly, half expecting to see something – he did not know what – standing behind him. But there was nothing there but the tree.

The following Thursday his mother had invited

some of the ladies from her watercolour class for coffee and Joseph had to say hello to them all and smile and be cooed at before he could make his escape. The day was dull and overcast, but the feathery grey clouds were high and would not bring rain. Joseph was the only thing moving as he strode purposefully across the open pasture towards the tree.

Joseph edged past the hole without looking in, and began his climb. He was surprised at how easy he found it this time as he quickly scaled the height he had reached the previous week.

When he reached the branch that marked the highest point of his earlier climb, he straddled it and sat feeling content and looking about him for signs of where he might find footholds for the next stage. He looked at his watch. It was only eleven o'clock. He had plenty of time.

It was then that he caught sight of the writing.

There, scratched into the trunk of the tree, where the branch he was sitting on sprung away from it, were the words, CLIMB NOT. They had been scratched into the bark in exactly the same way as the ones at the base of the tree. But these appeared to be freshly made.

Joseph stared at them and, suddenly feeling as if

he were being watched, he looked about him, out across the pasture. There was no one there.

Mr Farlow must have done this, Joseph was sure of it. The old man had warned him off climbing the tree after all. But could he really have climbed the tree at his age, however easy Joseph had found it?

Joseph suddenly laughed to himself. Of course! The old man did not need to climb. He had a ladder. Joseph had seen him at the top of a ladder the week before, pruning a climbing vine on the garden wall.

Then Joseph became angry. How dare that old man tell him what he could and could not do? What concern was it of his? He did not own this land – Joseph did. Or at least his parents did, and that amounted to the same thing after all. Instead of the words on the tree putting Joseph off, they became a spur for him to renew his struggles with even greater effort.

Joseph looked at the lettering of the words and smiled smugly. Why, the old fool could barely write; Joseph could have made a better job of that when he was four years old. And what had he used to make the letters anyway? Joseph had seen and admired the old man's knife that he kept in a sheath on his belt, but these words seemed to have been scratched with a nail or a hook rather than cut with a blade, as they were rough and jagged. Joseph felt the letters with his fingers. Whatever he had used it was certainly sharp, for the scratches were deep and the wood was as hard as stone.

Joseph saw that if he could crouch on the branch he was sitting on, he might be able to reach a branch that would then support him enough to stand and continue the climb. It was a precarious manoeuvre and, had he slipped, a broken arm would be the least he might expect in the resulting fall to the ground far below.

But Joseph managed to ease himself up on to the branch and, sure enough, he could reach out and grab a smaller branch above and pull himself up safely to a standing position.

From here the route suddenly seemed straightforward and Joseph climbed with ape-like ease, hauling himself from branch to branch with barely a pause to see where his next foothold would be. In no time at all he was pulling himself up to sit astride the very last set of branches that formed a kind of basket or crow's nest high up at the top of the tree.

Joseph whooped with triumph and gazed out at the view, out across the pasture towards the tiled rooftop of his house, which he now looked down upon. Looking to the west, he could see over the hedge to the fields and woods beyond and was able to discern very clearly the regular bumps and hollows that formed the imprint of a deserted village. The buildings were long gone, but their ghostly outlines could be detected through the blanket of soil and grass. He could even see now that the pasture, too, had markings in it. There were round markings every now and then and, stranger still, what seemed to be the remains of a pathway leading directly to the tree itself.

Then a flock of jackdaws croaked by, and Joseph was fascinated to find himself almost level with them. As they passed, Joseph looked up and saw something he had not noticed before.

Above him the tree died away, ending in a jagged stump, as if it had once been even taller, and in this highest part of the tree, embedded in the bark, were dozens and dozens of small metal objects.

Joseph stood up, his curiosity completely overpowering any fear he may have felt at the tremendous height. He stared in amazement at the treasure trove before him.

Hammered into the bark were crosses of silver and gold, bracelets distorted by the effort of forcing them into the wood, coins, rings and pendants from necklaces, brooches and buckles. Even Joseph could see that many, if not most, of these items were of great antiquity and must be valuable.

A gold brooch caught Joseph's eye. He reached out and grabbed it, giving it a tentative tug. It shifted a little. It had certainly been hammered in with quite some force, but with a bit of persuasion it would come free.

As he began to work it loose, he thought he heard a noise at the base of the tree and stopped. There were so many branches between him and the ground that he could not see anything but small patches of grass showing through gaps in the leaves.

He thought of shouting hello but did not want to alert anyone to his presence. If his mother caught him up here he would never hear the end of it and, after all, if he could not see them, they could not see him. He returned to prising the brooch free, and after a few seconds he had it in the palm of his hand.

This time there could be no doubt. Joseph distinctly heard a low moan, as if some kind of animal were at the foot of the tree, but no kind of animal he recognised – unless a bear had escaped from a nearby zoo.

Then it occurred to him it might be Jess; she might be badly hurt and moaning with the exertion of having dragged herself back.

'Jess!' he called. 'Is that you, girl?'

But it was not Jess. Whatever was making the noise was no longer at the foot of the tree, but had begun to climb it. He could hear the sound of something thudding into the bark and then dragging itself up, as if a soldier were scaling the tree using grappling hooks. He saw with mounting nervousness that the branches below him were shaking as whatever it was approached.

Joseph wondered if it was old Mr Farlow trying to frighten him, but even as he clung to this feeble straw of hope the thing swished into view. He could not make out any features on the black shadow that was climbing faster and faster towards him, save for the huge curved claws that it used to grip the bark.

The scream that Joseph made flew across the open pasture and crashed through garden wall and house wall and shattered the chattering peace of his mother's coffee morning. His mother instinctively ran towards the pasture, with her friends in tow. They found Joseph's body at the base of the tree, together with the branch he had been sitting on.

* * *

Joseph had a number of deep scratches on his legs and back, caused, they supposed, by the fall, and curiously his precious watch was missing and no amount of searching beneath the tree would uncover it.

'Elm's will drop their branches without warning,' said Mr Farlow, shaking his head when he heard the news. 'I did warn the boy not to climb.'

But Joseph's father decided to take vengeance on the tree he blamed for his son's death and demanded that Mr Farlow find someone who would cut the tree down. The old man shook his head.

'Not I, sir,' he said. 'And if I were you, I'd leave the tree be.'

There was something in the way the old man said the words that seemed to end the discussion and no tree surgeon was ever phoned. Instead, it was estate agents who were contacted and the house was put on the market once more.

They moved before the house was sold. Joseph's mother could not sleep there. The rustling of the great tree played on her nerves. Mr Farlow was kept on by them to maintain the grounds until a buyer was found.

At the very top of the tree, light would occasionally

twinkle as it played across the dented back of a watch embedded in the highest reaches of its ancient trunk.

'More tea, Edgar?' said my uncle, lurching forward rather alarmingly.

'Yes, please,' I said.

My throat did feel somewhat dry. I was finding it difficult to shake off the thought of being trapped at the top of that great tree with some name-less horror climbing inexorably closer and closer. My imagination had been horribly effective in its rendering of those murderous claws.

Uncle Montague refilled my cup and his own. He placed his saucer on his knee with one hand and lifted the cup to his lips with the other. When he had taken a sip, he put the cup and saucer back on the tray and got to his feet.

'Perhaps I should not be telling you such tales, Edgar,' he said, walking to the window and peering out. 'I do not wish to give you nightmares.'

'That is quite all right, Uncle,' I said. 'I promise you, I was not so very frightened.'

'Really?' said Uncle Montague, turning round

with a crooked grin. 'My tale was not frightening enough for you?'

'No, Uncle,' I said, putting my cup down with a rattle. 'That is to say, I mean . . .'

'Calm yourself, Edgar,' said Uncle Montague, turning back to the window. 'I was teasing you a little. Forgive me.'

'Of course,' I said with a smile. 'I realise that.'

Uncle Montague chuckled to himself but said nothing more. He seemed lost in a kind of reverie, gazing out through the windows to the garden.

I looked about me. The dancing fire flames were producing a not especially pleasant illusion of animation among the objects around the room and the shadows they cast. The shadow under my uncle's chair seemed particularly to have a life of its own and gave the unsettling impression that something was squatting beneath it, twitching and ready to dash out like a great spider across the room.

Though I knew, of course, that it could not be, the framed prints and paintings, the objects on the mantelpiece and on the cabinets, the books and the furniture – they all seemed to be trembling in anticipation, as if alive.

Uncle Montague turned and picked something up from the top of a cabinet nearby. The 'movement' of the contents of the study seemed to come to a sudden halt. When he turned back to face me I could just make out it was a tiny doll with a china head and fabric body.

My uncle walked over and handed me the doll with a degree of seriousness utterly at odds with the object, although I could see that it was made with unusual care. Still, it seemed an odd sort of thing for my uncle to have in his house. I felt a little foolish holding it and thought of the ribbing I would get at school should anyone there have seen me.

'Have you ever been to a seance, Edgar?' asked my uncle – a seemingly wild divergence from the doll he had so gravely placed in my hands. He sat slowly down in his chair.

'No, sir,' I replied.

'But you are aware of such things?'

'Yes, sir,' I said. 'People try to contact their departed loved ones. There are, I believe, those who claim to be able to allow spirits to speak through them.'

'Mediums,' said Uncle Montague, sitting down once more.

'Mediums, yes,' I added.

'You said "claim", Edgar,' said Uncle Montague.

'You are sceptical, then?'

'I have heard tell that there are those who say they have such powers, but who are fakers and conjurors, Uncle. I do not think it possible to speak to the dead.'

Uncle Montague smiled and nodded, tapping the ends of his fingers together and sinking back into the shadows.

'There was a time I would have shared your view,' he said, looking back to the window. I followed his gaze and thought I heard running footsteps outside on the gravel path by the window. Surely, I thought, the village boys would not dare to enter my uncle's garden.

My uncle had either not heard the noise or was untroubled by it, because he leaned towards me, smiling.

'I have a story on that subject that may interest you, Edgar,' he said. 'Perhaps it will change your opinion.'

'Really, Uncle?' I said, still feeling a little self-conscious holding the tiny doll. 'Please tell it, then, sir.'

'Very well, Edgar,' he said. 'Very well.'

The Un-Door

Harriet edged backwards towards the door as her mother began to speak. It was dark at the outer edges of the room, though it was only two in the afternoon. The heavy velvet drapes at the window blocked the light of day. The only illumination in the room was a lamp in the centre of an oval table, around which were seated eight women, whose expectant faces were lit by its greenish glow.

'Is there anyone there?' asked Harriet's mother in the odd trapped-in-a-well voice she reserved for these occasions, a voice that her clientele seemed to find haunting, but which Harriet always found faintly ridiculous.

'Are there any among the spirit world who wish to come forward and contact their loved ones here today?'

Actually, the truth was Maud was not Harriet's mother at all – and that was not the only lie they told, not by a long way. For one thing, Lyons was not Maud's real name; it was Briggs. They took the name Lyons at Harriet's suggestion – Harriet's own name was Foster – because it sounded more sophisticated.

They told people they were mother and daughter because it made them feel at ease. They had just enough of a familial resemblance to make it work, but in any case, as con-artists they knew that in the main, people simply accepted whatever you told them, provided it was credible.

Harriet and Maud had met in a workhouse on the Kilburn Road. They got the idea for the con when one of the other women told them about a seance she had seen her mistress host, when she had been a parlour maid. The maid had stolen from the guests and been caught and kicked out – hence her presence in the workhouse – but Harriet had seen straightaway that there was money to be made, if gone about in the right way.

They refined this piece of opportunism by taking control of the seance themselves. They advertised in one of the better ladies' magazines and presented themselves as experienced medium and doting daughter.

Spiritualism was all the rage and they found their gullible clientele needed very little convincing. It was Maud's job to commune with the spirits of the departed and while the ladies (and sometimes gentlemen) were busy listening to her wails and mutterings, Harriet would raid the coats and bags, taking small but valuable items that would not be readily missed.

If a pair of earrings or a silver snuff box was discovered missing a week later, the devout mother and daughter who helped contact their dear-departed loved ones would hardly be suspected of involvement. And even if they were, they would be long gone.

They had already decided that they should leave London for pastures new. Maud knew some people in Manchester. There was a lot of money up north. Another week or two and they would have changed their names and be buying their tickets at Euston station.

Harriet backed through the door and out into

the hall just as she had done in so many houses over the last months. She blinked into the relative brightness once she was out of the gloomy drawing room. The afternoon sun was streaming in through the stained glass above the front door and making a jewelled light on the walls.

Maud's voice seeped through the wall, tremulous and plaintive. Harriet smiled to herself and made her way back down the hall and up the stairs. The servants had been given the afternoon off at their suggestion, but she was careful as always not to enter the room above the seance in case a squeaking floorboard might alert one of the group.

She opened a door and peered in, ready to make her excuses about being lost if it was occupied. But there was no one in the room, which evidently belonged to children – girls, judging by the amount of lace and the enormous doll's house. It was certainly of no interest to Harriet, who quickly closed the door and moved on.

None of the rooms proved very interesting in fact. Mrs Barnard clearly did not trust her servants and had locked away anything of any value. Although Harriet had managed to lift a few interesting items and a little cash from the bags and coats of the women at the seance, it was hardly a

memorable haul.

As she returned downstairs, she saw two doors to her left that she hadn't noticed before and wondered if there might be anything worth investigating in them. She turned the handle of the left-hand door. Just as she did so, a voice behind her made her jump.

'I shouldn't go in there if I were you.'

Harriet turned to see a girl standing behind her, a little younger than herself. She was dressed in expensive, if rather old-fashioned, clothes.

'Hello there,' said Harriet with her most winning smile. 'What's your name, then?'

'Olivia.'

'Olivia?' said Harriet. 'That's a pretty name. Well, I'm sorry, Olivia. I'm afraid I was lost.'

'Lost?' said the girl with a little snort. Harriet did not much like her tone.

'Yes,' said Harriet. 'But the door was locked. I see now I came the wrong way.'

'The door is not locked, miss,' said Olivia, stepping closer in a way that Harriet found unaccountably threatening. 'It is blocked. We call it the Un-Door.'

'The Un-Door?' said Harriet.

Olivia nodded, smiling even more. 'That's what

we call it,' she said. 'Because it's a door, but it's not a door. Do you see?'

'Well, if the door is blocked, Olivia, why tell me I shouldn't enter?' asked Harriet, trying to retain her temper. 'I could hardly go through a door that is blocked now, could I?'

Olivia carried on smiling but made no reply. Harriet scowled.

'Anyway,' said Harriet, turning away. 'I must get on.' She walked towards the drawing room, in which the seance was taking place. She turned back as she opened the door, but the girl was gone.

Harriet re-entered the seance just as silently as she had left. She took a few seconds to adjust her eyes to the gloom and when she did so she could see Maud, staring ahead in a trance. Harriet had to admit it: Maud really did look the part.

Harriet glanced around the table – it was the usual mixture of the curious and the desperate: sad widows in their black clothes and jet jewellery, bored wives looking for a thrill. She stifled a yawn. Suddenly, Maud began to scream

'Please!' she shouted. 'Maud! For God's sake! Help me! Help me!'

The voice was so wild it made the whole room gasp and Harriet was as taken aback as anyone else

– especially to hear Maud using her own name. Harriet was momentarily rooted to the spot.

'Help me!' Maud screamed. 'For God's sake! Help me! Maud! Maud!'

Harriet pushed forward and grabbed Maud and tried to calm her down. Had Harriet not known Maud was a charlatan she would have said that she was possessed; her whole body seemed to be in spasm as if she had been struck by lightning.

'Goodness,' said an excited voice to her left. 'Is Mrs Lyons all right?'

'Quite well,' said Harriet brusquely, and indeed Maud did seem to be coming out of it. She blinked up at Harriet.

'Does anyone know a Maud?' said Mrs Barnard, looking round the table.

'What's that?' said Maud, startled at hearing her own name.

'That's right, Mother,' said Harriet, frowning at her. 'You were saying the name Maud just now.'

Maud stared back, confused.

'I think perhaps Mother has overtired herself,' said Harriet. 'Perhaps we should end it there.'

There was a groan of disappointment from the assembled ladies, but Mrs Barnard said that, of course, Mrs Lyons must not exhaust herself and that perhaps she ought to take a turn in the garden.

Harriet agreed and took Maud outside as the guests collected their things and began to leave, with Mrs Barnard thanking each of the ladies in turn. Harriet took Maud by the arm and led her away to a more secluded part of the garden.

'What the devil were you playing at in there?' hissed Harriet. 'You were using your own name, your real name! You trying to get us put away, you silly wench?'

'Don't you talk to me like that,' said Maud, still trying to shake off her wooziness. 'Or I'll . . .'

'Or you'll what?' whispered Harriet. 'You think I'm scared of you? Don't make me laugh. What were you up to?'

Maud shook off Harriet's grip and took a deep breath.

'I don't know,' said Maud sleepily. 'I don't remember. It was as if the voice was coming from somewhere else. 'Ere, you don't think I can really, you know . . . ?'

Harriet laughed. 'What? Really hear the bleeding dead? Are you on the gin again?'

Maud made no reply. She had a strange bemused look on her face and Harriet began to wonder if she was having some kind of seizure.

'Are you all right, Maud?' she asked, more annoyed than concerned.

'I don't know,' said Maud, turning to Harriet. 'I don't know.'

Harriet saw Mrs Barnard coming and nudged Maud in the ribs.

'Mrs Lyons, I must thank you once again,' said Mrs Barnard, walking towards them. 'The ladies all agreed that it was quite the most illuminating session we have had. Particularly when you were host to that poor creature at the end. Do you have any idea who she might be? We are all baffled.'

Harriet raised an eyebrow.

'No,' said Maud uncomfortably. 'I am afraid I do not.'

'It may have been a wandering spirit calling out for help,' suggested Harriet.

'Oh dear,' said Mrs Barnard, squeezing her hands together. 'Do you think so? The poor thing.' She shook her head sadly, her eyes closed as if in prayer. Harriet rolled her eyes at Maud, but Maud seemed to be staring off into the distance. The next moment she staggered sideways into Harriet's arms.

'Goodness,' said Mrs Barnard. 'I think Mrs Lyons is feeling faint. Won't you please come back inside?'

'No, no,' said Maud. 'I am sure I shall be quite well.'

'I must insist,' said Mrs Barnard. 'Perhaps a glass of sherry . . .'

'Yes,' said Maud, brightening at the thought of a drink. 'It is rather early, but perhaps just this once – for medicinal reasons.'

'What is the matter with you?' hissed Harriet as they followed Mrs Barnard back inside. 'You were supposed to keep her outside.'

'I don't feel quite right,' said Maud pitifully. 'Honest, I don't.'

'You ain't right in the head if you ask me,' said Harriet, suddenly smiling sweetly as she saw Mrs Barnard looking back towards them.

Mrs Barnard ushered them through the front door.

'Please go on in, Mrs Lyons,' she said. 'Sit yourself down and I shall fetch us some sherry. I would send for a doctor but the servants will not be back for an hour or so.'

'That won't be necessary,' said Maud, going for the nearest door handle.

'Not that one, Mother,' said Harriet. 'That door's blocked.'

'Blocked?' said Maud.

'Yes,' replied Harriet. 'The Un-Door they call it, I believe.'

Mrs Barnard stared at her in amazement. 'Now how would you know a thing like that?'

Harriet shifted uncomfortably, realising she had made a slip letting on that she had looked around the house while the seance had been in progress. *Never lie more than you have to,* she told herself. *The truth always sounds more convincing.*

'Your daughter told me,' Harriet said, in control once more.

'My daughter?' said Mrs Barnard, looking puzzled.

'Olivia,' said Harriet with a smile.

'Olivia?' said Mrs Barnard. 'You met Olivia?'

'Well, I had stepped out for a little air,' continued Harriet breezily. 'And I thought I might find a glass of water. I was trying the door handle when . . .'

'Olivia,' prompted Mrs Barnard.

'When Olivia appeared and told me that the door did not lead anywhere and told me that you called it the Un-Door.'

'The Under?' repeated Maud, becoming increasingly confused.

'The Un-*door*, Mrs Lyons,' said Mrs Barnard. 'And Olivia told you that? How clever of her. Please come this way.'

Mrs Barnard took them through to the room in which the seance had been held. The curtains were pulled back and daylight chased away all the atmosphere Maud and Harriet had painstakingly created for the benefit of the ladies. It had returned to being a rather ordinary, stuffy drawing room. Mrs Barnard opened one of the French windows to let in some air, then went over to the drinks cabinet and poured three glasses of sherry.

'Come with me, ladies,' she said, handing them a glass each. As she walked away Maud stared at Harriet with a questioning look, but Harriet merely frowned and followed Mrs Barnard back down the hall.

'Do you see how these two doors are evenly spaced?' she said. They nodded. 'Well, it seems that at some point many years ago they decided to take down a wall and open the two next-door rooms into one large room, as we have it now. I am told that they did not want to spoil the symmetry of the hall and so left this door here.' She indicated the left-hand one, then turned the handle of the door to its right. They followed her through.

'As you can see,' she said. 'The door – the Un-Door – does not appear on this side of the wall.'

Maud gave Harriet a slight nod of her head towards the cabinet nearby full of nicely concealable silver trinkets. Harriet nodded back.

'Come, I have something else I would like to show you,' said Mrs Barnard. 'That is if you are quite recovered, Mrs Lyons.'

'Me?' said Maud. 'Oh, I'm quite all right, my dear. You are so kind to be concerned. But we ought to be going really, shouldn't we, Harriet?'

'Oh, but you have time to see the doll's house?' she said.

'The doll's house?' said Harriet.

'I am really not sure we have . . .' began Maud, but Mrs Barnard was already leading them out of the room and towards the stairs. After a moment's pause they followed on behind.

Mrs Barnard led them up the stairs and opened the door Harriet had opened earlier.

'I'm sure Olivia will not mind,' she said.

'Oh, look, Harriet,' said Maud, feigning interest. 'Look at the doll's house there. I can't think I've ever seen one finer.'

'Yes,' said Mrs Barnard. 'It is a copy of the house we are in. The doll's house was here when our father bought the house in fact. We inherited it from the previous occupants.'

'It's beautiful,' said Harriet in genuine admiration. 'I would have loved a house like that as a child.'

Mrs Barnard sighed. 'I never liked the house to be honest,' she said sadly. 'I used to share this room with my sister – the house was really hers. She would play with it for hours. But there was something about it that rather gave me a chill. Still does actually.'

'A chill, madam?' said Harriet. 'Why?'

'Well,' said Mrs Barnard with a sigh. 'My sister became rather obsessed with the doll's house, I am afraid to say. She would sit in front of it like someone at prayer, muttering and mumbling. She would fly into a rage if I so much as touched any of the dolls. It was as if they were real to her.'

'But is that not true of all children, Mrs Barnard?' said Harriet.

'Yes,' said Mrs Barnard with a sad smile. 'But my sister was different from other children. She lost . . . all sense of reality. I suppose she lost her mind. I found her one day, laughing like a wild thing, huddled in the corner, wide-eyed, pointing at the doll's house. She never really recovered her wits. She became frantic and feverish, and no amount of laudanum seemed to calm her.' Mrs Barnard's eyes sparkled with tears as she turned to Harriet. 'In the end her heart simply gave out. She was only twelve.'

Harriet was surprised to feel a small pang of

sympathy for Mrs Barnard. 'It must have been very hard for you,' she said.

'It was,' said Mrs Barnard. 'It was. But it was a long time ago. Life moves on.'

Mrs Barnard turned back to the doll's house.

'As you can see,' she said, pointing to it, 'the doll's house shows the room downstairs as it was before the wall was taken down. In the doll's house, the Un-Door actually opens into a tiny room. Do you see?'

Harriet and Maud peered forward. The doll's house was indeed a rather good copy of the house in which they stood, the front wall and roof removed. There was the room in which they had held the seance, there was the hall, there was the bedroom they were in, complete, incredibly enough, with a tiny copy of the doll's house. And there was the room that no longer existed: the room the Un-Door had once led to. Harriet noticed that it had several tiny figures sitting in the chairs.

'This may help,' said Mrs Barnard, handing Harriet a magnifying glass. 'The detail is extraordinary.'

Harriet peered at the figures. There was something disturbing about them. Not only did the detail seem impossibly fine, but some of the figures had carefully painted features on their china heads and some had been left strangely blank.

'Well,' said Maud, growing a little concerned at the amount of time they were spending at the house. 'I think we should thank Mrs Barnard for showing us around . . . But we really must be on our way.'

'Of course,' said Mrs Barnard. 'I did not mean to keep you.'

'Is it still played with?' said Harriet as they were heading downstairs. 'The doll's house?'

'Oh, Olivia used to play with it all the time,' she replied. She stopped and turned to Harriet. 'Between you and me, I think she still does.' She reached out and touched Harriet gently on the arm.

Mrs Barnard followed them to the front door and out into the front garden. Just before they reached the gate, Mrs Barnard asked them to wait while she returned to the house for a moment.

'When she comes back out,' whispered Harriet. 'You keep her busy and I'll nip inside. I fancy a piece of silver from that cabinet we saw downstairs.'

'Right you are,' said Maud, tapping the side of her nose and winking.

Harriet shook her head.

'Are you tipsy, you old fool?' she hissed. 'You got

to keep your wits about you in this game. A couple of sips of sherry and look at you.'

'I could drink you under the table any day of the week,' Maud hissed back. 'Show a bit of respect.'

Mrs Barnard reappeared and they immediately pulled apart and stood smiling sweetly as she approached. She stood with them at the gate in the shadow of an enormous clipped holly tree and took a bank note from a pocket in her dress.

'Really, there is no need,' said Maud, taking it from her.

'For your expenses, Mrs Lyons,' said Mrs Barnard.

'Thank you,' said Harriet. 'You are very kind. Oh!' Harriet clutched her stomach and groaned.

'Miss Lyons?' said Mrs Barnard.

'I fear the sherry may have upset my stomach,' she said. 'I am not used to drinking. May I use your water closet?'

'Of course,' said Mrs Barnard. 'Let me show you . . .'

'No!' said Harriet firmly. 'Thank you. I will be quite well. I know where it is.'

Harriet hurried away, holding her stomach. Maud smiled in admiration.

'Poor girl,' said Mrs Barnard.

'Yes,' replied Maud. 'She is a delicate thing really.'

'I expect the excitement of meeting Olivia has something to do with it. I had not realised your daughter shared your gift, Mrs Lyons,' said Mrs Barnard.

'Harriet?' said Maud suspiciously. 'Gift? I am not sure I follow you, Mrs Barnard,' said Maud, growing concerned that, for all her apparent naivety, this woman was beginning to suspect something.

'But Harriet saw Olivia in the hall.'

'Your daughter?' said Maud puzzled. 'I fail to see how ...'

'I do not have any children, sadly,' said Mrs Barnard. 'Olivia was my sister.'

Maud frowned.

'I don't follow you, Mrs Barnard.'

'Olivia died when we were children,' said Mrs Barnard. 'As I told you upstairs. Harriet was blessed enough to meet and talk with her spirit.'

Maud looked from Mrs Barnard to the house and back again in utter amazement.

Harriet was surprised to see that the so-called Un-Door was slightly ajar. The whole story had been nonsense! But why – why would they lie about something like that? Perhaps she should have a quick look around.

As soon as Harriet opened the door and stepped in, she was blinded by dazzling light, bursting in from one side of the room as if it were a conservatory. She turned back to the door to leave. But when she grabbed the door handle it would not move. The door was locked.

Harriet turned back to the room to see if there was a connecting door to the other room or some other way out. When she did so, she saw a figure looming towards her out of the blazing light. Beyond her she could just make out other girls sitting in chairs about the room, staring horribly as if in a trance, their faces gaudily painted with rosy cheeks and arched eyebrows, slumped in stiff and awkward poses.

At first she had thought that she could not make out the features of the approaching girl because of the light behind her head, but now, with a terrible, falling feeling, as if she had stepped from a high cliff, she realised that the girl had no features to see. Harriet pounded on the door for help.

'Please!' she shouted. 'Maud! For God's sake! Help me! Help me!'

But that infinitesimal beat on the doll's house door was lost to everyone. Everyone but Olivia.

I was so gripped by my uncle's story that it was some time before I thought to look down at the doll he had placed in my hand before he began.

I brought the tiny figure up to my face and studied it afresh. The rosy firelight glow warmed up the features of the face and made the detailed painting even more startling. The features of the girl's face seemed impossibly, unfeasibly real.

'So, Edgar,' said Uncle Montague. 'Does that tale in any way alter your views on contact between the living and the dead?'

'Well,' I said. 'I would have to say that, respectfully, it does not. It is, after all, merely a story.'

'Merely a story?' said my uncle with a sudden violence that made me drop the doll into my lap. 'Merely a story? Is that what you think? That these tales are my inventions?'

'Well . . . yes . . . I rather thought they were. I am sorry if I have offended you, sir.'

'No, Edgar,' said Uncle Montague with a sigh. 'I am sorry to have snapped at you. What else would you think? I shall take that from you now.' He held out his long hand towards the doll. 'A lady does not like to be stared at.'

I gave him the doll and he walked over to the cabinet, putting it back where it had been. Again, he turned his back to me and looked out of the window. I could see that I had wounded his feelings in some way, but I was not sure how. Surely he did not expect me to accept these stories as true. How could they be?

'Come and look at this, Edgar,' said Uncle Montague.

He had moved over to examine a group of framed prints near the window. I got up to join him and as I walked towards him I had the strangest feeling that there was someone outside by the window, someone who ducked out of sight as I approached. I peered out but there was nothing to be seen.

My uncle was looking at a framed engraving of some sort of sculpture. It had the rather stilted quality of ancient engravings, but nevertheless it rendered its subject with enough skill to make it quite a startling image.

The sculpture itself took the form of a horned devil and even to my untrained eyes it had a medieval look about it. So it proved to be.

Initially I thought it was a gargoyle, as it was the kind of grotesque one frequently sees jutting out of a church tower, but on closer inspection I could see that the thing was carved in wood. I could also now see that it was part of the fabric of a church pew.

Quite why anyone – the original woodcarver or the engraver – would want to take the trouble to portray anything quite so odious was beyond me, but my uncle stared at it as if it were a portrait of a favourite granddaughter.

'Is the engraving valuable, sir?' I asked.

'The engraving?' said Uncle Montague. 'No, Edgar. It is not particularly valuable. It is the subject matter that is significant.'

'But what is it, Uncle?'

'Why, Edgar, it is a demon, of course.'

'Yes, Uncle,' I said. 'I meant to ask why it was so significant.'

'That is its significance,' he answered more solemnly. 'It is a demon.'

I waited in vain for my uncle to elaborate upon this opaque statement.

'Is there some story connected with this engraving, Uncle?' I asked, after the pause had become uncomfortably long.

'How perceptive of you, Edgar,' he said. 'But would you really want to hear another of my foolish inventions?'

'I have not called them foolish, sir,' I said. 'And I

would very much like to hear another of your stories.'

Uncle Montague chuckled softly and laid his hand upon my shoulder.

'Then let us sit down once more and I shall tell you a tale concerning our curious friend here.'

We returned to our chairs. Again, I could have sworn that I heard footsteps outside the window and the sound of whispering – of children whispering. My uncle seemed oblivious to it and so I took it to be my imagination, excited by my uncle's stories, playing tricks on me.

'But I wonder if this tale may be too disturbing for you,' said Uncle Montague, seeing me peering towards the window, turning to the fire and prodding at a log with the poker.

'Really, Uncle,' I said, pushing out my jaw. 'I am not as timid as you seem to think.'

Uncle Montague lay down the poker and turned to me with a warm smile – a smile that quickly faded from his face as he linked his long fingers together and began this new story.

THE DEMON BENCH END

Thomas Haynes first saw the tinker outside the bank in Sidney Street. His parents were inside, dealing with some dull financial matter, and Thomas was waiting in the street, watching the tide of Cambridge life flow past.

As he was standing there, the tinker shuffled by, dressed in a long frayed top coat and dusty wide-brimmed hat, his filthy hands gripping the spars of a rickety barrow, filled to overflowing with a seemingly random collection of rugs, clothes, shoes, scrap metal and broken furniture.

A rusting birdcage hung from a hook and chain,

clunking against the side of the barrow with every step the tinker took and Thomas was amazed to see a thin, bedraggled monkey, wearing a gaudy waistcoat and tiny red fez, suddenly emerge from under a blanket and come to the side to inspect him.

The tinker stopped in his tracks and turned to face Thomas. His eyes twinkled in the shadow of his hat and narrowed. A strange expression played across his face, as if he recognised him, though Thomas was sure they had never met.

Thomas was unnerved by this unwanted eye contact and was about to retreat into the bank when at that very moment his parents stepped out. They were about to walk on and go for lunch, when his father noticed the tinker's barrow still standing beside them.

'Good Lord,' he said, reaching towards something among the bric-a-brac. The monkey dashed towards him, baring his teeth and Thomas's father pulled back his hand.

'Filthy creature!' he hissed, shooing him away. The monkey ran chattering to the tinker, jumping on to his shoulder and staring back at Thomas's father malevolently. The tinker did not move.

'I say!' said Thomas's father. 'I say – you there!'

The tinker still did not move.

'The impertinence of the man,' muttered Thomas's father. 'You there!' he shouted, slapping the side of the barrow. The tinker flinched slightly and turned slowly round. His grim and unpleasant face wore the beaten and fragile expression Thomas had seen many times on his grandmother's face during one of her migraine attacks.

'What can I do for you, governor?' he said in a comically loud voice, as if he were calling from the other side of a river rather than two feet away.

'The poor man's clearly a little deaf, dear,' said Thomas's mother, putting her hand to her mouth to hide her smile.

'There's something in your cart here,' shouted his father. 'Your monkey . . .'

'Pablo won't hurt you, sir,' shouted the tinker. 'Don't be afeared.'

'Very well, then,' shouted Thomas's father, feeling a little self-conscious at the volume of their conversation. He reached in gingerly and grabbed a carved wooden figure. He held it up and inspected it carefully.

Thomas leaned forward. The carving resembled a rather elaborate bookend, fashioned into the shape of a horned demon with folded bat's wings, crouched on its haunches with its hand to its face in the pose of someone whispering, its long saturnine face frozen into a wide grin.

'What is it, Father?' said Thomas, fascinated and revolted in equal measure.

'I believe it to be a medieval bench end, Thomas,' said his father, turning it over in his hands admiringly. 'They sit at the end of pews in some old churches. Do you remember the ones we saw in Suffolk last year?'

Thomas remembered now. There had been elaborate carvings of animals and figures in medieval dress. But there had been nothing quite like this.

'Not for sale,' shouted the tinker.

'How did you come by this?' said Thomas's father imperiously.

'It's not for sale,' repeated the tinker even more loudly, already beginning to turn away.

'Do not adopt that impertinent tone with me,' said Thomas's father. 'I have a good mind to fetch a policeman!'

'It still won't be for sale,' said the tinker over his shoulder, pulling on the barrow and moving away towards the market.

'How dare you!'

'Rupert, please,' said Thomas's mother. 'You are causing a scene. People are staring.'

Thomas looked about and saw that people were indeed looking their way and two urchins, one with no shoes on his feet, were pointing and giggling. Thomas's father bristled, his face reddening, and he stroked his moustache with his thumb and forefinger a number of times before smiling at his wife.

'Very well, then. Who's for lunch?' he said, his humour restored, clapping Thomas on the shoulder as they walked on.

But over lunch, Thomas's father soon returned to the subject of the tinker and the demon bench end.

'What is the world coming to,' he said wearily, 'when something like that can simply be removed from a place of worship without any redress whatsoever?'

'It was rather ugly if you ask me,' said Thomas's mother.

'Grotesque, I will grant you,' said his father, 'but all the more fascinating for it. But he should not have it. It was part of the fabric of a church, darling.'

'And what about all those beastly things at the museum?' teased his mother. 'Were they not ripped out of temples and tombs and such like?'

'That's different, as well you know, my dear,' said his father. 'I hope you are not comparing my esteemed colleagues with that . . . that . . . odious beggar. He has no respect for such things. No respect at all. It is sacrilege, pure and simple.'

Thomas was surprised to find that despite the fact that he did not in any way share his father's interest in antiquities, he could not get the image of the bench end out of his mind. Long after his parents had moved on in their conversation, Thomas kept seeing in his mind's eye the hideous, leering face of the carved demon.

After lunch they walked past the venerable old colleges and out of town, through Newnham, out on to the river path back to Grantchester. Summer was coming to an end, but it was still warm and the countryside around them was bathed in September sunshine.

Thomas's parents walked the high bridleway, but Thomas himself kept close to the river, searching the weed-tangled waters for pike and excitedly watching a kingfisher flash by, exotically iridescent, like a jewel from a pharaoh's tomb.

Some rough village boys were clambering about in the branches of a tall tree on the opposite bank and stared at him sullenly as he walked past before renewing their games – one of them jumping from a dizzying height with a great splash in the middle of the river.

Further along, punts glided by, piloted with varying degrees of competence. Thomas looked at a group of laughing students sailing by and dreamed of the day that he might go to one of the colleges, whose high walls and guarded gateways he longed to breach.

But, once again, into the dreamy haze of these idyllic scenes the demon's grinning face returned and haunted him from every shadow and dark pool, until he retreated from the riverside and joined his parents on the ridge, craving company and the wide, bright view.

The following day Thomas was sent by his mother to take a note to the vicar about a musical evening she had been organising for some months. He had just walked past the church when he noticed the tinker's barrow they had seen in Cambridge.

Thomas felt a strange tightening in his chest. His hands suddenly felt a little numb and he flexed his fingers. Slowly, as if guided by a puppeteer, Thomas walked towards the rickety barrow.

The monkey sat at the back atop a pile of rolled-up rugs and eyed him with a haughty familiarity, as if he had expected to see him. But of the tinker there was no sign whatsoever.

Thomas edged towards the barrow, keeping a wary eye on the monkey all the time. He had seen the creature's teeth and he did not relish getting bitten. All the same, Thomas was unable to keep himself from looking for the carved bench end.

Sure enough, he saw the polished horns of the demon's head poking out from under a moth-eaten carpet bag. He looked around him. The street was as quiet as the nearby graveyard. All he had to do was reach out his hand and the bench end would be his. After all, this filthy tinker probably stole it himself. Stealing from a thief was hardly a crime at all.

But if he had no fear of the stain on his immortal character, then Thomas certainly had a very real fear of the monkey, who now seemed to regard him with utter disdain, as if he sat in judgement.

Thomas leaned forward, extending his arm and reaching his fingers towards the bench end. The monkey made no move to prevent him but sat looking straight into his face the entire time, until Thomas clutched the bench end to his chest. Feeling pleased with himself, he turned to walk away and came face to face with the tinker, who grabbed him by the arm.

The monkey suddenly let out a horribly loud and chattering laugh. Or at least Thomas had *thought* it was the monkey. But looking now, he could see that the monkey's mouth was firmly closed, despite the din. The tinker stared at him.

'I was just looking at it,' said Thomas. 'You can have it back!'

'Not likely, my friend,' said the tinker as the chattering grew in volume.

'Let me go or I shall call my father!'

'I'm sorry, my boy,' said the tinker. 'Very sorry. I mistook you for your pa. I never thought to be passing it on to a young fellow like yourself. But I don't make the rules. You'll see. When your time comes you'll be the same. You'll pass it on to your own mother if you have to.' An exhausted smile broke out across his face and he was panting as if he had just laid down a huge burden. Sweat was trickling down his forehead.

The noise was roaring through Thomas's ears. It sounded like a hundred thousand people talking at once: whispering, muttering, shouting and taunting. They talked over each other and drowned each other out, so that they blurred into one long stream of grating noise. Thomas was finding it difficult to hear what the tinker was saying.

'There are things you need to know, boy,' the man shouted over the babble of voices. 'So listen well.' He gripped Thomas's arm even tighter.

'You can't sell it,' he shouted. 'You can't give it away and you can't throw it away. Someone has to take it. They have to come to you. You have to make it as difficult for them as you can or it won't go.'

'What are you talking about?' yelled Thomas. 'Where is that noise coming from?' But even as Thomas asked he realised the truth. The noise was coming from the demon bench end.

'I found the damnable thing in the Kasbah in Tangiers twenty-two years ago,' continued the tinker, raising his voice even louder. 'I threatened to kill the fellow who had it if he didn't give it to me, and I killed him afterwards for passing it on to me, knowing what it was. But, of course, I know now that the demon will drive a man to do almost anything.' He stared at the bench end, his eyes flickering, wincing at memories he wished he could erase.

'I can't say why I ever wanted it in the first place, but it seems to choose us. I just knew I had to have it. I hope you get rid of it sooner than I did, lad, I really do.' Something like regret flickered across his weathered face, but only for an instant. He leaned closer to Thomas, but even so, Thomas had to strain to hear his words above the din coming from the demon. The voices were starting to synchronise now, as if they had all been saying the same thing all along, but out of kilter. Random words and phrases loomed in and out of the general cacophony.

'Don't listen to . . .'

'Weak, weak, weak . . .'

'Kill him . . .'

It made concentrating on the tinker's words increasingly difficult.

'If you love your family, then leave now,' he said. 'You'll hear things you won't want to hear. You won't know if they're true or not, but it won't matter; it will have poisoned everything. If you love them, get away – far away. He'll make you hurt them if you stay.' He stepped back, cocked his head sideways, making his neck click. 'Now if you'll excuse me, I must be on my way before that devil changes its mind.'

'Go on!' shouted the demon. The voices had now become one echoing whole. 'Run! Yes, run, you filthy, disgusting maggot! Run while you have the chance!'

The tinker turned and walked away, leaving the barrow where it stood. After a few moments, the monkey jumped down and scampered after him, scrabbling up and sitting on his shoulder, casting a backward glance at Thomas as he retreated into the distance.

Thomas looked down at the demon bench end as it screamed some disgusting accusation about his mother and Mr Reynolds from the library. Yet even as Thomas flinched at the creature's words, he was aware that he had always suspected something of that sort, though he could never have brought himself to voice it.

'You know it's true!' screamed the demon with a rattling laugh. 'But you could teach them a lesson. You could make them sorry. Those mouths that kissed, those lips that lied. You make them sorry, Thomas. They deserve to be punished. They deserve to choke on their filthy lies!'

Thomas put his hands over his ears but it made no difference. Old Mrs Patterson emerged from the porch of her cottage, blinking at the sunlight. She peered over the gate at Thomas. At first he thought her attention had been caught by the demon's screaming, but he quickly realised that she could no more hear it than Thomas or his parents could when the tinker was the victim of its torturous ranting.

It must have been the tinker's shouting that had brought Mrs Patterson to her garden gate and Thomas could see her concernedly mouthing something to him, but he could not hear her above the demon screeching about Mrs Patterson and a baby born out of wedlock – a child abandoned at a workhouse to die, neglected and unloved.

'Look at her, Thomas!' shouted the demon. 'She stands there like a saintly old maid, but she's just like the rest. I've been among people for hundreds of years and they are all the same, Thomas. They are all appearance, like an apple that hides the bloated maggot within.'

'No!' shouted Thomas, to Mrs Patterson's evident confusion. 'That's not true!'

'Thomas?' called Mrs Patterson. 'Are you quite well?'

'Listen to the putrid old sow!' shouted the demon. 'Why doesn't someone shut her up?'

Thomas turned away and ran helter-skelter out of the village and down the steep meadow that led down to the river, where cows lifted their heads and watched him with dull indifference.

When he reached the river he gripped the bench end in both hands, his arms outstretched. Its voice suddenly changed to a hideous whine as it pleaded with Thomas not to drop him in the water.

'Thomas,' it simpered. 'Please. I was jesting, that was all. That tinker was crazy, you could see that. I'm begging you not to drown me. Ple-e-e-ease.'

The wheedling tone was even more sickening to Thomas than the earlier sneering and he allowed himself a half-smile at his newfound power and at the realisation that the tinker had been plagued by this creature for over twenty years when all he needed to do was threaten to drown it.

Thomas relaxed his grip and the bench end fell, hitting the water with a satisfying splash. It floated down in a rocking zigzag path, disappearing into the darkness between the swaying weeds.

The braying voice of the demon likewise disappeared and Thomas was left with a deeper appreciation of the subtlety of the sounds that now greeted his ears: the rustling of the willow leaves, the flitter of dragonflies, the distant call of a magpie.

He looked about him and he felt a great swell in his spirits, as if he had been long confined in a cold grey cell and was now released, blinking and tearfully appreciative of the September sunshine and the beauty of the English countryside.

A light breeze played among the willows and far

away in the distance he heard the whistle of a train. He took a deep breath and looked down at the dark untroubled waters of the river. It was as if the beauty of the place had closed around the ugliness of the bench end.

Then, as Thomas watched, there seemed to be a movement among the weed fronds – an eel, perhaps, or a pike? There was something about its twitching and erratic movement that sent a shiver through Thomas's body and he turned away and began to walk back up the hill, speeding up as he did so, until he was quite out of breath when he reached the top. He looked back down at the river and smiled. Whatever the thing was, he was free of it.

It was then that he became aware of a noise – the sound of stifled giggles. Had some child been watching him? He must have appeared fairly ridiculous. He was about to call out for the child to show itself when he became horribly aware that his left hand was cold and wet.

With mounting horror he looked down and saw that he was holding the dripping bench end in his hand, a lime green strand of river weed draped about its neck like a scarf.

The demon could contain himself no longer and burst into a volley of cackling laughter. Thomas dropped it and ran, but he as he did so he was aware of the laughter getting louder and closer and he could once again feel the weight of the carving in his hand. *You cannot throw it away*, the tinker's voice echoed in his head.

'Oh, that's very good!' shouted the demon. 'That's well thought out, you brainless moron!' He chuckled throatily. 'Do you seriously think our rancid old friend the tinker would have suffered my presence for all those years if he could simply have thrown me in the nearest ditch? Oh no, little man. You don't get shot of me that simply, I'm afraid. The time must be just right. The next pilgrim who will have the gift of my company must be in place and ripe for the experience.'

'But why me?' cried Thomas.

'Do you know, they all say that?' said the demon. 'Why does the flea choose to bite one man and not another? How does the tapeworm choose one gut over another? Why not you? Would you prefer it to be your father, perhaps?'

'Yes!' shouted Thomas on the verge of tears.

'That's it!' shouted the demon triumphantly. 'Good boy! Why not that pompous old windbag? He is stealing from the university and yet he still has the effrontery to humiliate you in front of your mother over every trifling matter...'

'I never took that tobacco,' said Thomas.

'Of course not,' said the demon. 'But he wouldn't believe you, would he?'

'Is he really stealing from the university?' asked Thomas.

'Been doing it for years. But even that can't make him interesting. No wonder your mother is running off to disgrace herself with that reptile, Reynolds. But I am afraid that it does not work that way. I am yours and you are mine, and never the twain shall part; until a new host comes along. It is a curse, you see, and a curse must have rules or where would we be? Where would we be?'

Again the demon bellowed with laughter.

Thomas shook his head, closing his eyes and trying to shake off the dizzying effect of the constant noise. He was suddenly gripped by a steely resolve. Whatever the demon might say, Thomas was determined he would not share the fate of that broken and beaten tinker. This vile creature was not going to ruin his life. Of course he would say it was impossible to prevent it. Surely that was just what an evil hobgoblin like this *would* say.

Thomas strode off towards his house, ignoring the shrieks of the demon. He entered the back garden by the arched door in the high perimeter wall. Smokey, their cat, ran towards him across the lawn, but stopped in her tracks and hissed, fluffing out her long grey fur, as she saw the sinister bench end in his hand.

The demon launched into a screaming attack on the cat and its disgusting habits, gloating at the cancer it said was already growing in its neck. Thomas marched towards the shed, outside of which Benson, the gardener, had left his axe jammed into a huge hunk of beech.

The demon guessed where Thomas was heading and also his intent as he pulled the axe free. He screamed and goaded Thomas as he placed the bench end on the beech log and lifted the axe above his head.

'Go on!' it screamed. 'Go on! You haven't the nerve, have you, you spineless piss-in-the-bed? Look at you! Your hands are shaking! You're pathetic! *Pathetic!*'

Thomas took a deep breath and slammed the axe head down with all his might, closing his eyes as it struck home.

But instead of silencing the demon, Thomas's blow had merely resulted in more raucous laughter. When he opened his eyes it was not the bench end that lay split by his axe, but Smokey's body, and he dropped the axe as if it were on fire and turned his face away in horror, tears welling in his eyes.

'Oh, diddums!' shouted the demon. 'Is little Tommy's pussy-wussy broken, then? Do you know I think you may have taken her head right off? That's one catnap she won't be waking up from!' The demon cackled and Thomas found that the bench end was back in his hand.

'Leave me alone!' shouted Thomas, bursting into tears.

'Oh dear, oh dear,' said the demon. 'I can't do that I'm afraid, Tommy boy.'

Thomas sobbed.

'Come on,' said the demon. 'I can't believe you are crying over that damned cat. Good riddance to the nauseating fleabag. You never even liked her, admit it!'

'I did!' yelled Thomas. 'I loved her!' But even as he said it, he wasn't sure.

'No, you didn't,' said the demon with a chuckle. 'Not really. Not at all. The truth is, you don't really love anyone, do you, Thomas? Not really. Not even yourself. Isn't that true?'

'Stop it!' yelled Thomas.

'Tommy, Tommy, Tommy,' said the demon. 'Calm

down. It's all a shock to you, I know. You want your old life back, I understand that. But it's gone. It's gone for good.' The demon's voice dropped to a hiss. 'And why? It's all that filthy tinker's fault, isn't it? He tricked you. If it wasn't for him, everything would be as it was. He's the cause of everything! He ought to pay and pay dearly. Why people are hanged for less – much less – and yet he gets away with ruining your life. Anyone would understand if you took the law into your own hands and taught that filthy old man a lesson ...'

Thomas nodded slowly. The demon was right about that at any rate. That pig had ruined his life. He would work out some way of ridding himself of the demon later.

'He's slow. He's weak,' screeched the demon. 'You can catch up with him in no time.'

'I don't even know which way he went,' said Thomas.

'Yes, you do,' said the demon. 'Of course you do. He's walking the green lane to Trumpington. You can cut across the fields. It's a quiet route. There will be no one about.'

After a moment's pause, Thomas began to move towards the garden door.

'You're going unarmed?' screamed the demon

incredulously. 'A boy like you against a crazy old man like that? He has a knife, remember. Didn't you see it hanging from his belt? You need some protection. He's killed before, you know.' The demon laughed. 'Oh yes – many times, many times. I've seen him do it.' The demon chuckled.

Thomas looked at the axe.

'Good, good,' screeched the demon. 'That's good thinking. Come on! Come on! He's getting away.'

'I can't carry you and the axe,' said Thomas.

'The gardener has a canvas bag in the tool shed. Put me in that!' cackled the demon.

Thomas's ears were stinging from the demon's onslaught. The demon's voice had wormed it's way into his brain and Thomas found it difficult to distinguish which were his thoughts and which were the demon's promptings. He found it hard to think about anything but the tinker and the heavy axe that he now held in his hands as he ran, head bowed and teeth clenched, towards the open fields.

I took a sharp intake of breath when my uncle finished, as if I had been underwater for a little too long.

'I wonder what the demon would say to me, Uncle,' I said, expecting my uncle to say something comforting along the lines of, 'Those without secrets or wicked desires would be safeguarded from its attentions.' Instead he leaned forward and held both my hands in his. His face was ashen and there was a haunting earnestness about his expression.

'Pray that you never know, Edgar,' he said, his eyes fixed on mine. 'Pray that you never know.'

'Yes, Uncle,' I said, prising my hands gently from his grasp and getting to my feet once more. I must confess that at this point I had begun to have some concerns about my uncle's mental state. He seemed to be in danger of losing his ability to distinguish between the real and the imaginary.

I walked across to the framed engraving again and took another look. Having heard Uncle's story, the grotesque features and leering expression of the wooden demon seemed even more sinister than before, if that were possible.

At that very moment, I heard the faintest of creaks and, looking round, saw that the door handle was slowly turning.

'Go away,' said my uncle, so quietly and matter-of-factly that at first I thought he might be talking to me.

The door handle stopped and then, after a pause, began to turn again.

'Leave us!' said my uncle with more force this time. The handle rattled as it was released.

I had assumed that our visitor must have been Franz coming to see if his master required any further assistance, but it seemed to my ears that more than one pair of feet moved away down the hall and I was sure that I had once again heard whispers.

'Does anyone else live here, Uncle?' I asked tentatively.

'Live?' said my uncle oddly. 'No, Edgar.'

A log fell from the grate on to the hearth with a splutter and crackle and the potency of the fire's glow suddenly faded. It was as if all the shadows in the room reached out towards me. Out of the corner of my eye I fancied I saw the demon in the engraving move.

I forced myself to study its gruesome features once more, but it remained resolutely immobile, as I knew it must. I smiled to myself at my foolishness.

'Come away, Edgar,' said my uncle quietly. 'There are some things that should not be looked at too much.'

'Yes, Uncle,' I said, humouring him in this fanci-
ful conceit.

There was a small oil painting nearby, over-
powered by a heavy moulded frame of mahogany
or some such oppressive wood. But the painting at
least was a more attractive image than that of the
demon bench end.

I am no great judge of paintings, and certainly
had no real appreciation of the arts as a boy, but
this seemed rather fine, though the varnish had
darkened with time and rendered the scene – a fine
house and gardens – somewhat more sombre perhaps than originally intended. The gardens to the
rear of the house in particular were almost black. I
could just make out the signature: A. Trewain.

'It was painted by a young doctor,' said Uncle
Montague from his armchair. 'He had real talent, I
think.'

'It has a strange atmosphere,' I remarked.

'Yes,' said Uncle Montague. 'Yes, it does. Come
and rejoin me by the fire, Edgar, and I shall tell you
why.'

The vicarage of Great Whitcot in Suffolk was a rather grand house, built in the 1750s, of warm marmalade-coloured bricks and pantiles. The house bulged forward in two curved bays and the windows of this bow front were tall and wide, separated into a grid of smaller, white-framed panels that looked out on to the gravelled driveway and the orchard plot with its fallen walnut tree. Between them nestled a claret-coloured door with white columns either side.

The grounds of the house were girded all around by a brick wall of such height that it created its own twilight in the areas of the garden that fell into the gloom of its shadow – a gloom only deepened by the towering beech trees at the back of the house.

The wall was pierced in only two places: by a small arched door leading into the graveyard of the enormous and very fine medieval church, and by the entrance to the drive, where the wall curved gracefully down to the two pillars bearing large stone spheres.

Robert Sackville took all this in as he stood by one of the pillars, watching his father marshalling the men who were shuffling back and forth with furniture, boxes and trunks from the large wagon parked on the dirt road beyond the gate.

Robert's mother scurried about, gasping and calling out as chair legs struck doors and the sound of broken glass came tinkling from the morning room. Robert's father stood relatively impassively – his hands behind his back, one slapping the back of the other as was his wont – only becoming animated when the men began shifting boxes of his precious books, shepherding them to the library and watching their every move like a hawk.

Robert, as usual, felt superfluous to proceedings and wondered to himself just how long it would be before anyone would notice were he to simply walk out through the gate and across the field of swaying barley beyond.

He drifted aimlessly towards the gloomy rear of the house, picking up a willow wand left by the gardener, and flicking it through the air with a whistle. As he walked to the back door he stopped, suddenly struck by a feeling that he was being watched. He peered into the shadows but could see nothing. He swished the willow wand again but nothing moved. With a shrug Robert opened the door and went in.

No sooner had the furniture been placed in the appropriate rooms than a procession of locals crocodiled down the drive, holding baskets and parcels wrapped in muslin or old newspapers.

'Oh dear,' sighed Robert's father. 'I suppose this is my flock.' He shook his head wearily and went to open the front door as the head of the crocodile reached the steps. Robert went to his bedroom window and looked down.

Hats and caps were snatched from heads and clasped to chests as his father opened the door. Robert could hear muffled conversation through the thick window panes and saw his father self-consciously take possession of the various gifts being offered. Robert's mother appeared in the doorway and heads were bowed respectfully as she thanked them all for coming.

'God bless you all,' Robert heard his father say and there was a succession of bows and nods and near-curtseys from the ladies and then hats were replaced and brims tugged in farewell before the delegation crunched its way back down the gravel drive and out of the gate.

'Merciful heavens!' Robert's father was saying as Robert came downstairs. He recoiled from a news-paper parcel that lay, half unwrapped, on the table in the hall. Robert went over to have a closer look as his father backed away. There was a dead rabbit in the newspaper. A note was pinned to the fur, saying: *Well come to Whitcot. Fresh kild this morning.*

'Oh my Lord,' said Robert's father. 'I daren't open the others.'

'Don't be silly, Herbert,' said his mother. 'I think it is very thoughtful of them. The rabbit will be delicious and look, here's a plum pie and there's some honey. You must be sure to thank them in your sermon. They do not have so very much, Herbert. This is very generous.'

'What on earth is all this?' said Robert's father, peeping suspiciously under a layer of muslin and into a wicker basket.

'I rather think they are offerings,' said a voice

behind them. Robert, along with his parents, turned at the sound of the voice to find a tall man in his forties standing in the doorway, hat in hand, dressed in a tweed suit, a wide grin shining out from under a thick black moustache that curved up to meet his sideburns.

The man introduced himself as Arthur Trewain, the local doctor.

'I live on the other side of the village. I was just passing and thought I ought to say hello.'

Robert's father stepped towards him and shook his hand.

'Reverend Sackville – Herbert Sackville. Pleased to make your acquaintance, Dr Trewain,' he said. 'May I introduce my wife?'

'Mrs Sackville,' said the doctor, taking her outstretched hand. 'It is a pleasure to meet you.' He turned and looked at Robert, whom his father clearly had no intention of introducing.

'And this must be your son,' he said.

'Yes,' said his mother. 'This is Robert.'

'How do you do, Robert,' said Dr Trewain, holding out a hand, which Robert took and shook. 'I expect you shall find us a little dull. There are no suitable boys for you to play with, I'm afraid. Young David Linklater is about your age, but he is in

London for the rest of the holidays.'

Robert said that he would be quite all right – there were only two weeks left of the holidays and then he would be back at school. Dr Trewain smiled, nodded and then retreated backwards out of the door, saying that he should really let them unpack. 'If you need anything,' he said as he replaced his hat. 'Please do not hesitate to ask.'

'Perhaps you might like to come to dinner?' said Robert's father.

'I would like that very much,' said the doctor.

'Of course, you must,' said Robert's mother. 'And is there a Mrs Trewain, may I ask?'

'You may,' said Dr Trewain. 'But there is not, sadly. I have never found anyone willing to take me on. The life of a doctor's wife is not to everyone's taste.'

'Nor the life of a vicar's,' said Reverend Sackville with a smile and a sigh. 'I count myself very lucky indeed to have such a wife as Elizabeth.'

'And so you should,' said Mrs Sackville with a laugh. 'What do you say to coming over on Friday evening?'

'I would be honoured,' said the doctor.

The next few days moved horribly slowly and Robert counted the hours until he was to return to school – to escape, to be himself. He longed for the company of other boys. He felt uncomfortable about the village and not just because he was a newcomer.

Being the vicar's son was a burden he had shouldered all his life, but it became no easier to bear for all its familiarity. It was as if, by being the son of a man of the cloth, he was expected to behave as if it were a family business he was about to inherit.

But Robert had no interest in following his father into the Church. He wanted to live his own life, to steer his own course. Besides, though he could never, never have brought himself to tell his father, the fact was he simply did not believe in the God his father had pledged his life to serve.

Dr Trewain certainly seemed to be right about the dullness of the village. There were no 'suitable' children to play with, and even the unsuitable ones seemed disinclined to visit the vicarage or its environs. So Robert moved listlessly about the garden, regressing into some of his old amusements: looking for nests among the shrubs and hunting for bugs among the terracotta pots and edging stones of the drive.

But he was always drawn back to the rear of the house – to its permanent and dreamy twilight.

Perhaps the very fact that it was shunned by the adults, even the gardener, made it seem something he alone possessed.

Then, one afternoon, to his surprise he saw a boy – a well-dressed boy – sitting on the high wall that stood almost invisible among the shadows under the trees.

'Hello,' said Robert.

The boy made no reply, but he leaned forward and his face widened into the broadest grin Robert had ever seen and Robert, feelingly instantly at ease, smiled back.

The following day – Friday – Dr Trewain duly arrived in the early evening, holding a small bunch of flowers in one hand and a rather fine bottle of port in the other.

'Not too bored, I hope, Robert,' said Dr Trewain as they all sat in the parlour.

'Not at all, sir,' said Robert. 'I have made a friend after all.'

'A friend?' said Dr Trewain, a little surprised. 'Really?'

He was about to ask the identity of the friend when they were interrupted by Jenny, the maid, calling them into dinner, and over the meal the

subject of the villagers and their 'offerings' was raised.

'They are good people, sir,' said Dr Trewain. 'And they are just deeply grateful to have a new vicar.'

'Was my predecessor so very unpopular, then?' asked Reverend Sackville cheerfully.

'No, not at all,' said Dr Trewain. 'Reverend Benchley was much loved and greatly respected . . .' His voice trailed away.

'Yes?' said Robert's mother, sensing the doctor was not quite telling them everything.

Dr Trewain smiled sadly and told them that towards the end of his life, Reverend Benchley had changed somewhat and that his death was preceded by bouts of rather unpredictable behaviour.

'Poor man,' said Mrs Sackville.

'Unpredictable in what way, may I ask?' said Robert's father.

Dr Trewain sat back in his chair.

'I am afraid that Reverend Benchley was subject to a kind of morbid obsession. He was a bachelor, as you know. I think perhaps he had spent too much time in his own company. I know a little of the way that can shape a man's thoughts.'

'You said a "morbid obsession", Dr Trewain,' said Mrs Sackville. 'An obsession with what exactly?'

'An obsession with a notorious previous occupant of this house,' he replied.

'The house had a notorious occupant?' said Mrs Sackville. 'I'm intrigued, Doctor.'

Dr Trewain apologised, saying that he had assumed that the bishop might have mentioned something of the vicarage's past history.

'Please, do go on,' said Mrs Sackville. 'I promise I will not be shocked. Vicars' wives are a fairly unshockable lot.'

'Very well, then. I suppose there's no harm –'

There was a sharp knock at the door and Jenny the maid entered.

'Beg' pardon, sir, madam, but there's a lad come from a Mrs Hunter, whose been taken terrible bad and needs Dr Trewain urgent.'

'I'm terribly sorry,' said Dr Trewain. 'I will have to go, I'm afraid. Mrs Hunter has been very ill of late.'

'Of course,' said Reverend Sackville. 'We must go where and when our work takes us, Doctor. We are alike in that respect.'

Dr Trewain nodded, and thanking them for the meal and their company, he hurried away.

Saturday was overcast, and Robert had to concentrate just to see that his new friend was there at all in the gloom under the trees.

The boy had not asked, but Robert knew what it was he wanted and Robert surprised himself at how eager he was to do the boy's bidding. Robert had always been a leader rather than a follower, but he now felt different somehow.

Robert had seen a large plank of wood standing near the greenhouse that would be perfect for the job. The boy nodded and his smile lit up the darkness like a lamp.

Later that evening, Dr Trewain dropped by to apologise for having left in such a hurry the night before.

'How is the patient?' said Mrs Sackville.

'Not so good, I am sorry to say,' he answered with a sigh. 'Mrs Hunter is a very sick woman.' Dr Trewain was disconcerted to see Robert grinning, and he frowned. Mrs Sackville followed his gaze.

'Robert?' she said crossly. 'I cannot see what there is to be so happy about.'

'Oh,' said Robert. 'I'm sorry. I was thinking about something else.' Mrs Sackville stared at her son. There seemed something strange in his manner. Reverend Sackville interrupted the silence to ask Dr Trewain what he had been going to tell them about the house. Dr Trewain took on the look of a man who, having said a little too much, knew he would not be allowed to end it there.

'Fear not,' he said. 'It is ancient history; in fact not even history – more hearsay and rumour and tall tale. I would not have mentioned it at all were it not for the fact that the villagers have long memories and it does have some bearing on the last days of old Reverend Benchley. But perhaps it may be a little disturbing for some ears.' He cast a meaningful glance at Robert, and Robert's mother nodded.

'Time you were off to bed, darling,' she said.

'But, Mother,' protested Robert.

'Come along now, my boy,' said his father. 'Do as your mother says.'

Robert half closed his eyes and took a deep breath.

'Very well, Father,' he said, getting to his feet. 'Good night.'

'Good night, darling,' said his mother.

'Good night, Robert,' said Dr Trewain.

'Good night, sir,' said Robert with a little bow, before turning and leaving the room.

Robert climbed the stairs. He did not care about their silly secrets. The tedious history of this house was of no concern to him. He heard his mother apologising for him and he smiled to himself. What did he care what they thought about him. What did he care what they thought about anything?

On Sunday morning Reverend Sackville conducted his first sermon, which went well – Mrs Sackville noticed out of the corner of her eye that there were many appreciative nods and murmurs when the service came to an end. Dr Trewain shook the vicar warmly by the hand and congratulated him as they stood in the sunshine outside the church porch.

Robert stood nearby and stifled a yawn. He peered up at the wall above their heads at a row of lichen-encrusted gargoyles, each one more grotesque than the last. One of them, a strange grinning creature near the tower, seemed oddly familiar.

'Where have you been?' asked Robert's mother when he walked into the drawing room the following day.

'In the garden, Mother,' he said. 'Do you know where there's a hammer?'

'A hammer?' said his mother with a laugh.

'Yes,' said Robert matter-of-factly. 'And some nails.'

'No,' she said with another laugh. 'I'm afraid I do not, darling. Why on earth do you ask?'

'I need them, Mother,' said Robert, frowning.

'Well, perhaps Mr Fenner will know . . .'

But Robert was already walking out of the door.

Mrs Sackville sighed and returned to the book she was reading but realised she was no longer in the mood. She had a sudden craving for the excellent port Dr Trewain had brought, but was terrified that a servant might find her drinking alone at eleven o'clock in the morning.

She found the constraints of being a vicar's wife every bit as frustrating as Robert found those of being a vicar's son. She loved her husband dearly and he was very supportive of her views on female emancipation, but she hungered for more.

Mrs Sackville had been surprised at how affected she had been by Dr Trewain's revelation about the history of the house. She had been expecting him to recount some ancient scandal or impropriety and had been completely unprepared for what was actually related.

She was a rational woman at heart and ordinarily the tale of the late Reverend Benchley's obsession with a previous, sixteenth-century vicar, who supposedly dabbled in sorcery, would have intrigued rather than disturbed her. She had often toyed with the notion of writing a study of English folk tales and this would have made an excellent subject. But disturbed her it had. There was something about this house that allowed the idea of someone conjuring up a demon – as this Reverend Rochester was supposed to have done – to seem horribly plausible. She understood, too, how in the weakened state of old age, the Reverend Benchley's mind could have become unnaturally fixated upon this tale; how he might have convinced himself that the demon still haunted the darker recesses of the house and grounds.

Even so, she smiled to herself. She refused to become that kind of silly woman who starts at every floorboard creak and sees hobgoblins in every shadowed corner. The repetitive beat of hammering came from outside and she walked through to the hallway at the back of the house and looked out of the window. Robert had evidently found a hammer. What on earth was he up to?

Mrs Sackville did not like the darkened patch of garden and she noticed that neither the maid nor the cook, nor indeed Mr Fenner the gardener, ever seemed to go there. Only Robert frequented that area; only Robert and the big old cat he seemed to have adopted as a playmate.

It was curious, the change that had come over

Robert. He seemed to have retreated into himself since they moved here. He had always been something of a secretive child, content in his own company, but it was almost as if he had taken refuge in the kind of childish make-believe she had assumed he had long grown out of. But there was also something strange in his manner. The sooner he was back in school, the better.

Mrs Sackville watched her son. She felt a little guilty at so doing, for she had always believed him to have as much right to privacy as any adult. And yet, it was so fascinating to observe him going about his play with that earnest industriousness peculiar to children.

So taken was she by this idealistic notion that it was a few minutes before another impression began to register. Robert was wielding the hammer he had borrowed with a kind of fevered relish. What was he doing?

He seemed to be taking nails from his lips the way she had seen workmen do, and was struggling in his efforts to nail something – something that Mrs Sackville saw squirming in his hand as he struck.

Mrs Sackville felt a giddy feeling flutter in her stomach and she moved to the garden door. As she opened it, the sound of Robert's hammering could be heard more sharply.

'Robert?' she called, standing in the doorway.

He made no reply but took another nail from his mouth and hammered it home.

'Robert!' she called again, annoyed at how her voice cracked at this greater volume. 'Answer me this instant!'

Robert hesitated mid-blow, turned and faced her; then grinned and continued. This brazen insolence riled even the mild-mannered Mrs Sackville and she stepped through the open door and began to stride across the patchy back lawn towards her son.

'Robert!' she demanded as she approached. 'Robert! How dare you ignore me? What are you doing there?'

Robert got slowly to his feet and turned. She had not noticed before how tired he looked. There were dark stains under his red-rimmed eyes and his skin had a sickroom pallor to it. As she approached, Robert stood back from his handiwork, the better for his mother to see.

On a long plank of wood supported at either end by two upturned terracotta pots was the most extraordinary collection of creatures.

In the dreamlike clarity of that first glimpse, Mrs Sackville could see beetles, worms, a frog or toad – she could not tell which – crickets, flies, butterflies, a mouse and several birds, one of which was still twitching horribly. They were all pinned or nailed to the plank and, judging by the twitching bird, had been alive when Robert fixed them there.

'Good God, Robert,' she said. 'What have you done? What monstrous thing have you done here?'

Robert smiled horribly and she noticed that his attention seemed to be distracted. She followed his sideways glance to the wall at the back of the garden. There was something there. The mangy old cat was trotting towards them along the top of the wall.

'He is my friend,' said Robert, and then sensing that he had not given sufficient weight to this statement, he winked and said, 'my *special* friend. I have done all this for him.'

Mrs Sackville stepped forward and slapped Robert hard round the side of the face, so hard that Robert had to take a step back to steady himself and Mrs Sackville was shocked to feel how much her own hand hurt. Robert rubbed his cheek and looked away to the wall.

'What are you talking about?' said Mrs Sackville, suppressing a sudden urge to vomit and following his gaze. 'You are trying to say you did all this to please a cat?'

'A cat?' said Robert, genuinely confused.

'Yes,' said his mother. 'A . . .'

But she could see now that it was no cat, but something else – something not at all right. What she had taken for fur, she could see now was more like spines of some sort and this only partly covered its body, leaving patches of warty and raw-looking skin elsewhere. The head looked like something partially skinned and cooked.

Mrs Sackville's mind struggled to cope with what she was seeing as the creature leaned horribly towards her, its impossibly wide mouth opening and closing as if in silent speech. She lifted her hand to her chest to aid the flow of breath that was now coming so painfully slow. She clutched at the linen collar, at the cameo at her throat. The pin at its back pierced her thumb almost to the bone but she did not feel it. She dropped unconscious to the ground.

Robert was momentarily aware that he should have been upset to see his mother lying on the ground at his feet, her dying breath leaving her pale lips, her eyes still wide open, but he was not.

He looked up at his friend sitting on the wall and his friend's mouth broke into one of those remarkable, warm, generous smiles. And Robert, once more, smiled back.

A heavy silence followed the end of Uncle Montague's story, interrupted only by the ticking of the clock. I pulled my clammy hands apart and wiped them on my trouser legs as my uncle leaned forward out of the shadows, the rosy firelight warming his face.

'I trust I am still not frightening you, Edgar,' he said, raising one eyebrow.

'No, Uncle,' I said, my voice sounding surprisingly small. 'Of course not.'

Uncle Montague walked slowly to the window and pulled aside the curtain, the milky winter light throwing him into silhouette. I wandered over to the painting and peered into the murky depths behind the house. Was there something there? A boy? There did seem to be something, but what it was I could not have said for sure.

'It looks as though a fog is closing in, Edgar,' he said.

'Really?' I said, going to join him by the window.

Sure enough, the wood and paddock had disappeared altogether and the garden was likewise being erased by lace-like swirls of fog, curling among the topiary and statues. It was strange to see the suddenness of its arrival, for there was not the least hint of such weather when I arrived. Then something seemed to move between the topiary bushes.

'What was that?' I said, pointing to the place I had seen it.

'What do you think it was?' said Uncle Montague.

'I could not say,' I replied. 'It moved so quickly.'

'The fog is full of such phantasms,' said my uncle as if that were an end to the matter. It was unclear whether he meant fog in general, or this fog in particular. Either way, I was not keen to venture out into it.

'I hope it clears before I go home,' I said.

'Yes,' said Uncle Montague. 'We would not want you getting lost.'

'That would never happen, Uncle,' I said. I was sure I knew the journey blindfolded.

'Really?' he said, sounding surprised. 'There are

many ways of getting lost, Edgar.' His face seemed suddenly touched with sadness and he patted me on the shoulder. 'Let us return to the fire. This damp air gets into my bones.'

I realised that I too felt a sudden chill gripping my body and I leaned forward and warmed my hands against the fire's welcome heat.

'Are you feeling cold, Edgar?' asked my uncle.

'Yes,' I answered. 'A little.'

'The fog has crept in, I think,' said Uncle Montague. 'And there is nothing like fog to chill the soul. I'll ring for Franz and he can bring us a fresh pot of tea. A hot drink should revive you.'

Franz was duly called and a new pot of tea was brought together with another plate of biscuits and a refilled sugar bowl. Uncle Montague put the tray on the table between us once more and poured us both a cup.

'This is no entertainment for a lively young fellow like yourself, Edgar. I'd warrant you would rather be climbing trees or playing rugby.'

'Not at all,' I said. After Uncle Montague's story about the elm tree I rather thought I might never climb a tree again. As for rugby, it was a game I had always detested.

'Do you have no friends then among the local

boys?' he asked. 'Would you not rather be getting up to mischief somewhere?'

'Mischief, Uncle?' I said. 'I am not very good at mischief, and besides, the local boys are rather childish. I would rather be here, sir.'

Uncle Montague smiled.

'Very well, then,' he said.

'Were you mischievous, Uncle?' I asked, seeing a chance to glean some information about my enigmatic relative. 'When you were a boy?'

Uncle Montague raised an eyebrow. 'When I was a *boy*?' he asked. 'I should hope that I am not yet too old for mischief.' Uncle Montague leaned towards me, grinning.

'Come now,' he said. 'Is your existence really so *angelic*, Edgar?' He placed such a disapproving emphasis on the word 'angelic' that I was tempted to invent some bad behaviour simply to please him. Uncle saw my struggles.

'Never mind, lad. There is no shame in being a good boy,' he said with very little conviction.

'No, Uncle,' I said, having never for one moment ever thought that there could be.

'Perhaps you would like to hear a cautionary tale about a boy whose behaviour was not quite so commendable as your own, Edgar,' said Uncle

Montague finally.

'Yes, Uncle. I would like that.'

'Excellent.' He flexed his long bony fingers, his face becoming a mask of seriousness once more. 'Excellent . . .'

Winter Pruning

It was a crisp, bright October morning. Yellow and brown leaves were slowly falling through the chill air. Frost shimmered in the shadows.

A boy called Simon Hawkins leaned on the cold damp wall, staring at the old woman in the garden beyond. Though Simon could see her, she could not see him, for Old Mother Tallow was blind.

The children in the village called Old Mother Tallow a witch and dared each other to knock on her door. None had even mustered the nerve to enter her garden. On Halloween they threw eggs at her house and ran away. Simon had wandered there in a moment of boredom to see if blind Old Mother Tallow was up to anything exciting. It seemed unlikely.

She wore a grey coat with a thick shawl over that. A heavy dress fell all the way to her feet, the edge of which was soaking up the dampness from the grass. She wore black boots and fingerless gloves. She had a woollen bonnet on her head and her face was red with the cold.

The old woman was examining one of four old apple trees in front of the house. Simon studied her with the same sort of fascination he would were she a bee or an ant going about its business.

She was running her sinewy fingers over the trunk and branches with one hand while opening and closing a pair of secateurs with the other. She reached a point at the end of one branch and raised the secateurs, closing the blades round a twig and cutting into it. As she snipped through it a flock of redwings took flight from a nearby holly tree.

'Who's there?' she said suddenly, making Simon jump. Her voice was low and whispered and yet it seemed to crack like a whip in the silence of the garden. Simon did not answer.

'Come,' she said, without looking round. 'I may be blind, but I'm not deaf – or stupid. If you have come to frighten an old woman, then shame on you.'

'My name is . . . Martin,' said Simon.

'*Martin*, is it?' said the old woman with what sounded to Simon like doubt in her voice. But how could it be doubt? How could she know any different? 'And what do you want, Martin?'

'What are you doing?' he said.

'Pruning,' said the old woman. 'I am pruning my apple trees. If I did not prune them they would not give me such delicious apples. They would waste all that energy growing new branches and leaves. They need to be tamed.' As she said the word 'tamed', the secateurs yawned open and quickly snapped shut. 'Now I ask you again: what do you want?'

'Nothing,' he said defensively.

'Nothing, is it?' she said. 'I know you children and your greedy clutching little fingers.' Simon was a little taken aback by the sudden venom in the old woman's voice.

'I'm not doing anything,' he said.

'Then go away.'

Simon did not move.

'Go away,' she said again.

'Why should I?' said Simon. 'I'm not doing any harm. I'm not even in your garden. I'm not scared of you.' It was a brave boast that was not helped by the tremble in his voice.

The old woman turned and began to walk towards him. Her eyes were as frosted as the grass on which she trod. There was something so horrible about the gaze of those clouded marble-like eyes that Simon found he could not bear it. He pushed himself off the wall and ran down the hill back to the village, laughing nervously to himself when he was well clear.

Simon was bored. He and his mother had recently moved to the village from the city and to the house that had been his mother's childhood home. Simon's grandfather – his mother's father – had died, leaving them the house and the hardware shop that went with it. Simon's own father had been killed fighting for his country in a far-off land when Simon was a baby and their life had not always been easy. His mother thought the move might give them both a new lease of life.

'Do you know anything about Old Mother Tallow?' said Simon as he and his mother ate lunch.

'Old Mother Tallow?' said Simon's mother with surprise.

'Yes,' said Simon. 'The blind old bat up the hill.'

'Simon, really,' said his mother. 'Up at the top of Friar's Lane, you mean? But she can't still be alive.

Why she must have been a hundred when I was a little girl. Mind you, she can't have been, because my mother could remember teasing her when *she* was a girl.' His mother stopped and stared into space. 'Wait a moment. That cannot be right, can it?'

'Well, there's an old lady there,' said Simon. 'And she's blind and that's what everybody calls her.'

'Maybe it is a daughter,' she said. 'How odd. They used to say she was a witch, you know.'

'They still do,' said Simon with a grin.

'We were terrified of her,' said his mother. 'We used to call her names and run off.' She shook her head at the memory of it and blushed a little. 'Poor woman. How horrible children can be.'

'Speak for yourself,' said Simon, grabbing an apple from the bowl and taking a bite. 'Why were you so scared of her?'

'Because of her being a witch, of course,' she said, laughing to herself. 'Honestly, the nonsense we used to come out with! They used to say she was immensely rich – though if she was, goodness knows why she was living alone in that tiny cottage – and that she captured children who came into her garden and ate them.'

'Ate them?' said Simon, chuckling.

'Yes,' said his mother with a mock growl. 'Ate

them or threw them down a well or something awful! We were terrified! You know, I can still see her standing in the front garden with those two creepy old apple trees beside her. They used to say that the apples were delicious, but how anyone knew I don't know, because they also said that once you took one step on to the lawn she flew at you like a crow and pecked out your heart.'

Simon laughed and his mother couldn't help but join in. 'I mean it,' she said. 'I was very scared of her. The way she seemed to look through you with those awful eyes of hers.'

'But she's blind,' said Simon.

'I know,' said his mother with a shudder. 'It makes no sense, but there you are. I had nightmares about her.'

'There, there,' said Simon. 'I'll protect you.'

'You won't go up there, will you?' she said.

'Scared I'm going to get pecked?'

'Of course not,' she said, slapping him on the arm. 'But you won't, will you?'

'No, Mother,' he said with a sigh. 'I won't. I promise.'

Simon was not quite the child his mother took him for, however, and this promise, like so many other promises he had made, meant little. Simon's ears had pricked up at the mention of the idea that the old lady might be rich. He was sick of stealing pennies from his mother's purse. He was tired of hearing how little money his father had left them.

The following day he walked up Friar's Lane once again. He raised himself up on to the wall and swung his legs over. He sat there looking at the cottage with its broken-backed roof and lichen-covered tiles, its tiny windows peeping out of climbing roses and honeysuckles, and the unkempt lawn with the gnarled, arthritic old apple trees, twisted and deformed by years of pruning.

Simon smiled when he thought of his mother and her nightmares about this twee old cottage and the crabby old crone who lived there. He stretched out a toe towards the lawn and rested his foot there. A blackbird suddenly fluttered past and he snatched his foot back.

Simon shook his head at his own childish jitters, took a deep breath and hopped down as silently as he could. As soon as his feet hit the grass, the old woman appeared at the garden door, like a spider reacting to a movement in her web.

'Who's there?' she said.

Simon held his breath. Old Mother Tallow edged out of the door, cocking her head to one side with the effort of listening. Her eyes seemed to glow like cat's eyes.

Then it occurred to Simon that perhaps the old woman did this every time she left the house, merely as a precaution, and that it was a coincidence that he was there. She was an old blind woman living on her own. It made sense to check that everything was all right before she left the house.

After all, how could she have heard him from inside? In any case, she seemed satisfied there was no one there and began to busy herself at one of the apple trees. When she snipped through a twig, birds took flight once again – wood pigeons this time – noisily wheeling overhead.

The old woman had left the door open and Simon saw his chance. The grass was long and he found that he could move in silence. His route to the door took him horribly near the glass-eyed old woman, but she seemed oblivious to him as she squeezed the secateurs in her bony hands and cut through another twig. The blades flashed in the sunlight and slipped through the flesh of the wood with a loud SNIP and there was something hideous about the relish Old Mother Tallow seemed to take in this cutting. Simon turned away and walked on.

As he walked through the front door he was

filled with relief at having eluded the old lady, but this feeling was immediately replaced by one of mounting unease.

He was now in a small house whose layout he did not know. What if the old woman came back inside? What if she tried to attack him? He thought of the secateurs and their flashing blades. What if she was as mad as everybody said?

Simon shocked himself with the matter-of-fact way he picked up the walking stick, but he reassured himself that hitting the old woman would be a last resort. A weapon made him feel more relaxed and he began to look around.

What Simon saw was a disappointment. If Old Mother Tallow was rich, she did not seem to spend her money. The furniture was old and threadbare. A layer of dust and cobwebs covered everything in sight.

The cottage may have looked like a fairy-tale witch's house from the outside, but inside it was mundanely shabby. There was a smell of damp and though a fire burnt in the lounge grate, it seemed colder inside than out. Simon could see his own breath and rubbed his hands together to get some warmth back to his fingers.

He looked around the tiny rooms downstairs

with a growing sense that he was unlikely to find anything of value. He lifted cushions from chairs and looked in vases and under ornaments, but there was no sign of any cash or valuables. The kitchen was equally disappointing.

He crept upstairs. He had heard about old ladies stashing money under their mattresses, but not Old Mother Tallow. A search under her sagging mattress unearthed nothing but a hairgrip and two dead woodlice.

Wardrobes, chests of drawers and linen baskets all failed to deliver any riches. Even a promising-looking jewellery box held only a tinny-looking old brooch. Simon caught sight of himself in the dressing-table mirror as he rooted through the old woman's things and a tiny pang of guilt troubled him for a second, but he shook it off with a smile.

Simon crept downstairs again and was about to leave when he noticed in the little hall by the door there was a strange wooden box on a low polished table. It startled him and made him look about and listen for Old Mother Tallow, because he was sure it had not been there before. But when he peeked through a window, the old lady was standing in the same patch in the garden, snipping away at the tree.

The box was made of a reddish wood and seemed

to be the only thing in the house not covered in a layer of dust, as if the old woman polished it every time she walked past.

Simon picked it up. It was warm to the touch. There was a carving on the lid, a carving of the front of the house he was in with the lawn and the apple trees. He noticed that when the box was carved there had been five apple trees rather than the four outside. There was even a carving of Old Mother Tallow herself, pruning the trees just as she was doing in the garden outside.

It was a curious thing. The scene was at once crudely rendered and amazingly realistic. As he moved it in his hand, the light played across the polished surface and gave the strange sensation of movement, as if Old Mother Tallow's movements in the garden were being mirrored in the wooden box.

Simon opened it up and whistled silently to himself. The box was packed with crisp £1 notes. They looked brand new, as if they had never been touched. So it was true. The old witch really did have a secret hoard. Simon grinned wolfishly.

He took the money out and stuffed it into the inside pockets of his coat and zipped it up again. He replaced the box and began to leave. Out of the corner of his eye he thought he saw a movement in the carving on the box.

Simon walked out of the house and was comforted to see that Old Mother Tallow was still at work on the trees. He smiled and set off for the garden wall, gently patting the bundles of notes inside his coat.

But he hadn't taken two steps across the lawn when a blinding flash lit up the garden as if a huge but soundless firework had been detonated next to him. The world went white and he felt himself pass out.

When he came round he was still in Old Mother Tallow's garden. He seemed to have woken up on his feet, but whatever had knocked him out had done something to his vision. He could see, but in a different way from before. He had a panic that he had been horribly hurt somehow. He could not feel or move his face.

He wanted to run, but when he tried to move he found that he could not. It was as if he were rooted to the spot. In fact, not only could Simon not move his feet, he seemed unable to move any part of his body. He could look out across the lawn towards where he had been sitting earlier, and he was dimly aware that there were branches to the left and right of him. He seemed to be tied to one of the apple trees.

Simon was cold too. The chill breeze seemed to go straight through him. Had the crazed old woman stripped him? What had she done to him? What was going on? He wanted to struggle but was unable to move at all.

He was aware of a bird landing on one of the branches nearby, but felt it as though it had landed on his bare forearm. He could feel with excruciating sensitivity the prick of its tiny claws as it edged along, then hopped and scurried to the end of the branch. He felt the grip of its feet as though on his own fingers, flexing and squeezing as it shifted its weight before flying off as Old Mother Tallow appeared.

It was then that Simon realised the truth of what had happened, though his mind struggled to accept it. He was not *tied* to an apple tree. He *was* an apple tree.

'Now then,' said Old Mother Tallow, opening and closing the curved blades of the secateurs with one hand and feeling along his arm-branch to his finger-twigs with the other. 'I think we will need to do a lot of work on you. A *lot* of work.'

Simon let out a scream – a long and painful scream that only the birds could hear – and a flock of startled finches took flight, flapping wildly above the old woman, the cottage and the five gnarled apple trees.

I realised when Uncle Montague had finished his story that I had been sitting on my hands as if to protect them in my imagination from those vicious secateurs of Old Mother Tallow. When I took them out from under my thighs I had lost all feeling in them.

I shook them and wiggled the fingers and Uncle Montague smiled, pouring us both another cup of tea. I wondered aloud if the fog was still as thick as it had been and my uncle said that I should go to the window and take a look.

I was amazed to see, when I pulled back the curtain, that the view was now utterly blank – as if the whole world had been erased and my uncle's house floated in a void. It was an unpleasant and strangely dizzying sensation and I quickly closed the curtain to shut it out.

As my uncle jabbed a poker into the fire I took a stroll about the room. It was full of such an amazing array of extraordinary things that no matter how many times I looked round it, I never felt I saw the same thing twice.

Then I happened to look at a nearby bookcase and saw on one of the shelves a wooden box whose carved decoration I immediately recognised from the story I had just heard. I reached out a hand to touch it, but before I got there my hand seemed to flinch involuntarily and I found that I could not do it. I wondered if my uncle had a story about everything in this room.

My eyes fell upon an elaborate gilt frame hanging on the wall and I was surprised to see that it was empty. It seemed an odd thing to hang on the wall. My uncle suddenly appeared at my side.

'You have noticed the gilt frame,' he said.

'But why is it empty, Uncle?' I asked.

'Ah, yes,' said my uncle, nodding sagely. 'Why indeed?'

I had hoped that my uncle might continue and answer this question, but, as so often, he felt no need to say anything further.

'Is the frame a family heirloom?' I asked, gently probing for more information.

'No, no,' he said. 'Like most of the objects you see in this room, it has simply come into my possession over the years.'

'You are a collector, Uncle?' I asked. I hoped

that at last I was going to hear something of my mysterious relative's own history.

'Of a kind, Edgar,' he said. Again my uncle felt no need to elaborate.

'It must be an expensive pastime,' I said coaxingly. I could tell that though few of the pieces Uncle owned were what one might call beautiful, some of them were clearly valuable.

'No, Edgar,' he said. 'They were given to me.'

'They are all gifts?' I said, gazing round and wondering why my uncle should have been the recipient of so much generosity.

'Of a kind, yes,' said Uncle Montague with an odd wry smile. I obviously looked a little confused.

'As you must realise by now,' he continued, 'these things around us are – how shall I put it? – possessed of a curious energy. They resonate with the pain and terror they have been associated with. My study has become a repository for such items. I am a collector of the unwanted, Edgar, of the haunted, of the cursed – of the *damned*.'

I was not altogether happy with the way my uncle looked at me as he said this.

'But, Uncle,' I said, 'you speak as if the events in your tales actually took place.' Uncle Montague's eyes glittered and his eyebrows rose. I felt that I was being teased and I could feel the colour rise to my face. 'But how could that be possible?' I asked. 'And how could you know, sir? You could hardly be a witness to all these events and it occurs to me that in most cases the principal character in the story is hardly in a position to tell their tale.'

My uncle smiled and held up his hands in defeat.

'As you wish, Edgar,' said Uncle Montague. 'As you wish.'

I confess I was rather pleased with myself for having stood my ground. My uncle walked to the window, pulled open the curtain and stared resolutely into the fog. I saw his lips moving, though I heard nothing. It was almost as if he were mouthing something through the window to someone outside. I could see no one there, but then the fog was so all-encompassing that there might have been a crowd of suffragettes and I should not have seen them. It was troubling that my uncle appeared so distracted, and again I grew concerned.

'Perhaps it is time you were running along home, Edgar,' he suddenly announced.

My heart sank. The fog, as I have said, was as thick and uninviting as ever, and besides, I did not want to leave my uncle in such a strange mood. I wondered if I could repair the damage my questioning had done by coaxing my uncle into telling another of his stories.

'I was wondering, sir,' I said.

'Yes, Edgar?'

'About the gilt frame?' I said, pointing to it. 'I was wondering in what way it was "cursed" or "damned" or what have you.'

'Were you indeed?' he said, turning to face me with a grin. 'But surely you have had enough of a foolish old man's ramblings for one day.'

'Not at all, sir,' I said. 'Rather . . . that is to say . . . I do not think you foolish, sir.'

'I am glad to hear it, Edgar.'

Without another word, we both walked across the room and returned to our chairs by the fire. Uncle Montague raised his hands to his face as if in prayer and then lowered them to his lap, leaned back into the shadows and began his story.

THE
GILT
FRAME

Christina and her sister Agnes scampered excitedly down the stairs on hearing their mother return. Mrs Webster had been up to London to visit the family lawyer and there was every chance that she had bought them a gift.

'Now, girls,' she said, as they ran towards her. 'I can see by your faces that you are expecting a gift and you really must not. Mr Unwin says that it is high time we started to live within our means. He is a horrid, impertinent little man, but until circumstances change, we should do as he says.'

'Are we poor then, Mama?' said Agnes.

'Of course we are not poor, Aggy,' said Christina. 'Don't be so foolish.'

'Not poor,' said their mother, handing her coat to Eva, the maid. 'But we are far from rich, my chicks, far from rich.'

'What's this, Mama?' said Agnes, picking up a bundle that was leaning up against the wall. Christina eyed it excitedly; perhaps their mother had bought them something after all.

'Oh, that,' said their mother with a sigh. 'Oh well. Your Aunt Emily insisted that I accompany her to a small auction in aid of . . . in aid of . . . well, in aid of some poor unfortunates whose need is greater than ours and, well, I came away with this.' She tore away a corner of the bundle and revealed an ornate gilt frame.

'It was a bargain, actually,' said their mother. 'Worth the price for the frame alone. But, girls, you must let me get on. I have no end of things to do before dinner and I really must take a nap. Talking about saving money does tire one so.'

When their mother had gone, Christina clenched her fists and stamped her foot, hissing a complaint about her mother's soft-heartedness.

'How could she spend our money on such rubbish? She cannot even remember whom the auction was for. Our money will probably go to some awful people who are only poor because they don't want to work. Penelope's father says London is full of them.'

Eva tutted loudly and shook her head.

'Your mother is very kind woman,' she said. 'Shame on you.'

'How dare you criticise me,' hissed Christina. 'I suppose you think it's very amusing that we are to be paupers.'

'You do not know the meaning of being poor,' said Eva.

Christina opened her mouth to reply, but Agnes interrupted.

'Leave Eva alone, Chris,' she said. 'It's not her fault mother didn't buy us a present.'

Just at that moment their mother reappeared. She had a curious knowing look on her face and Christina was sure she had been listening. She picked up the bundle and took the rest of the wrapping off.

Christina gazed pleadingly up at her mother and asked if she could see. Inside the gilt frame was an old studio portrait photograph. It was of a girl about her own age with dark hair and a Mona Lisa smile. What on earth had possessed her mother to buy such a thing?

'Would you be a dear, Eva,' she said. 'And hang it for me? It can go over there in place of that dreary watercolour.' Christina remembered how her mother had bought that dreary watercolour at a similar auction the year before.

'Of course, madam.'

'Thank you, Eva.'

With that, their mother left to take her nap. Eva busied herself taking down the watercolour and replacing it with the photograph, walking away towards the kitchen when she was done. Agnes said she was going to finish a letter she was writing to their grandmother and disappeared upstairs.

Christina was left alone in the hallway feeling a seething rage against everyone in the household, when she heard a whispering coming from nearby. She looked about her, but there was no one. Then she realised the sound seemed to be coming from the photograph in the gilt frame.

'Over here,' it said quite clearly.

Christina's heart skipped a beat and she backed away to the other side of the hall, bumping painfully into the table. The girl in the photograph giggled.

'You needn't be frightened,' she said.

'W-w-what are you?' Christina stammered.

'I will be your friend,' said the girl. 'If you'll let me.'

'My friend?' Christina frowned. 'What do you mean? You're a photograph and I must be dreaming or feverish or something.' She put her hand to her brow.

The girl in the photograph giggled.

'I have the power to grant you three wishes,' said the girl. 'There must be something you would like.'

'I must be dreaming,' murmured Christina, pinching herself. 'I must be.'

'What are you doing?' said a voice behind her, making her jump. It was Eva. The girl in the photograph was a mere photograph once more.

'I was not doing anything,' snapped Christina. 'And in any case I can do as I like. This is my house.'

'This is your mother's house, I think,' Eva said, smiling and walking back towards the kitchen.

'So?' said the girl in the photograph. 'Is there nothing you wish for?'

'I wish that stupid Eva would leave me alone!' hissed Christina.

As soon as she said the words she felt a curious sensation, as if there had been a sudden change in air pressure. She felt light-headed and put her hand on the banister to steady herself. She blinked a couple of times to focus, but saw that the photograph was static once more. She clicked her fingers in front of the girl's face, but nothing moved.

Christina laughed nervously to herself. Perhaps she was coming down with something, after all. Could she really have hallucinated the whole thing? She shook her head and blinked again. Already the idea of it being a trick of her mind was easier to believe than that a photograph had actually talked to her. She laughed again.

The family were having dinner some days later when the doorbell rang. The girls looked at each other in wonder. No one ever called at this hour. Their mother frowned and stood up, wringing her napkin nervously.

'Now whoever can that be?' she said.

Eva had answered the door and they could hear a muttered conversation going on in the hall. Mrs Webster left the room and after exchanging wide-eyed glances, the girls followed her.

They found Eva in tears. The door was open and there were two stern-looking gentlemen in dark overcoats on the doorstep and a policeman standing behind them, looking back into the street.

'What on earth is going on?' said their mother. 'What is the meaning of this? Eva? What is the matter?'

'I am afraid Miss Lubanov must come with us, madam,' said one of the stern gentlemen. Christina took a moment to realise that he meant Eva.

'Go with you?' said Mrs Webster. 'But why? I really must protest ...'

'Please,' said Eva. 'It is better I go. You have been so very kind, ma'am. I do not wish you to get in trouble for me.'

'Listen to her, madam,' said the other man. 'She does not have the correct papers and she must go. You will only make trouble for yourself if you interfere.'

'Eva!' cried Agnes and she rushed forward to hug the maid. Eva had stopped crying now. She hugged Agnes and cast a hard glance over at Christina.

'Please, madam,' she said. 'Do not try to help me. You must look after yourself.'

'You poor dear girl,' said their mother, hugging her. With that, the men took her away and ushered her into a waiting carriage. In seconds they were gone.

When her mother was upstairs consoling Agnes,

Christina lurked about at the parlour doorway, working up the courage to step into the hall alone.

'You have come for another wish?' said the photograph.

Christina stepped nearer.

'I did not wish for Eva to be taken away,' said Christina. 'I only asked that she would leave me alone. It's not my fault that she was taken away.'

The girl in the photograph smiled. 'And your second wish?'

Christina did not like the way she spoke to her. It was almost as if she *did* blame her, but was choosing not to say anything. After all, if she could grant her anything she wanted, Christina was hardly going to argue with her, but this time she was going to wish for something rather more useful than the absence of an irritating maid.

'I wish we were rich,' said Christina with the imperious raise of an eyebrow she had seen her friend Penelope employ to such effect.

There was no reply from the girl. In fact there was no sign that the photograph had ever been anything other than simply that: a photograph. Christina walked away to wait and see what would happen.

Day after day went by but nothing changed. She

had almost given up on seeing her wish fulfilled when the telephone rang one rainy Saturday afternoon.

Christina's mother had her back to her as she took the call and seemed to have to steady herself at one point, her hand clutching the back of a chair. She replaced the receiver and stood, head bowed, in silence for a moment.

'Mother?' said Christina.

Mrs Webster turned to face her daughter, tears in her eyes.

'Go and fetch Agnes, dear,' she said.

Christina did as she was asked and their mother took them into the parlour.

'It's Grandmama,' she said. 'Be brave, my chicks. I'm afraid . . . I am so sorry, but she has passed away.'

The news hit Mrs Webster especially hard, coming as it did so soon after Eva's deportation. Her mother-in-law could be a cold woman and had used the promise of her money as a kind of weapon, but she had been Mrs Webster's last link to her dear husband, Robert, who had died so long ago the girls could barely remember him. Christina was left feeling cold.

Later, when Agnes and Christina were alone

together, Agnes said sharply, 'You never did like Grandmama!'

'She did not like *me*!' replied Christina.

Agnes shook her head in exasperation.

'You shall not make me feel guilty,' said Christina. 'I am sorry Grandmother has died but, unlike some, I shall not pretend to be upset.'

Agnes took a sharp intake of breath and slapped Christina round the face with all the strength she could muster. The blow was sharp and stung Christina's face, bringing tears to her eyes and knocking her sideways on to the bed. When she looked up Agnes was gone. She rubbed the side of her face and ground her teeth together.

'I'm sick of her,' she muttered. 'I wish I had my own room.'

The word 'wish' echoed in her head. Had she really wished her own grandmother dead? No. She had wished for the family to be rich, that was all. True, her grandmother's death did now mean they were rich, but that was hardly her fault. She was not to blame for how the wish was made real. When she looked up again her mother was standing in the doorway.

'Dear Christina,' she said with more than a trace of surprise in her face and voice. 'Why, you are crying, sweetness.'

'Yes, Mother,' she said. 'Poor Grandmama.'

'She is with the angels now, God rest her soul,' said her mother.

'How did she die, Mama?' asked Christina, sitting up. Her mother looked away for a moment and clenched and unclenched her fingers.

'She had a fall, my darling,' she said. 'I had warned her so many times about that staircase but she would not . . .'

Christina's mother closed her eyes and took a deep breath. When she opened them a tear ran down her cheek. Christina got up from the bed and ran over to her mother, hugging her. Her mother stroked her hair and Christina clung on tightly, rejoicing in this new closeness between them.

Perhaps it was not too late to make amends. Christina had had a small taste of what it must feel like to be good, to be Agnes, and she liked it. Maybe it was not too late for her to change.

Agnes came back to the bedroom a little later to find Christina still sitting where she had left her. To her surprise, Christina opened her arms wide and said how sorry she was.

'Can you ever forgive me, Agnes?' she asked.

'Of course I can,' said Agnes, embracing her.

'You're my sister. And I should not have hit you.'

'I deserved it,' said Christina. 'I was being beastly. I've been beastly for a long time but I'm going to change, Agnes, I promise.'

The two girls clung tightly to each other until Agnes said that she felt tired and lay down on her bed. Christina sat by her, stroking her hair until she fell asleep.

Christina was suddenly aware of a harsh ringing sound – a sound she took a little while to identify as the doorbell. The room seemed to have become suddenly darker. How long had she been sitting there? She went dreamily to the landing to see Bertha, the new maid, answering the door.

Christina looked down the stairs as Bertha, looking very serious, went to fetch Mrs Webster, leaving two dour-looking men standing on the doorstep.

Christina's mother went to the door and, after a good deal of talking, showed the men through to the morning room. Christina tiptoed downstairs. She wondered who the men were, but only for a moment. It did not matter. Nothing mattered.

She stood in the hall and edged towards the photograph in the gilt frame. She knew exactly what she would wish for. She stood in front of the girl and the girl smiled back.

'You do not look very happy,' she said.

'I wish,' said Christina, ignoring the girl. 'I wish that everything was as it was before my mother brought you back from the auction.' Christina closed her eyes as she made her wish, but opened them almost immediately when she heard the girl giggle.

'You look silly,' she said.

'Why haven't you granted my wish?' said Christina with a frown.

'I have granted you three wishes, as I promised,' said the girl. Like a flash of lightning exploding in her head, Christina remembered her wish to have a room of her own and a scream rang out through the house, hanging in the air like gun smoke.

The morning-room door burst open and one of the men ran through, followed by Mrs Webster. They ran pell-mell up the stairs as Bertha appeared on the landing, screaming once again and pointing hysterically. The second man stood over Christina, an odd expression on his face, his hands clenched and the muscles of his jaw twitching.

Christina could hear footsteps and muffled voices coming from her and Agnes's bedroom. Why was that silly maid screaming so? She put her hands over her ears. Then she saw the photograph in its gilt frame. It became suddenly clear what she had to do if she was going to keep her promise to Agnes, if she really was to be a better person.

Christina lurched forward and grabbed the photograph, smashing it against the banister. The crash shocked the maid into silence. Christina's mother stood at the top of the staircase and gasped as she saw her daughter standing in the hallway, the gilt frame in her hands and shards of glass strewn about the floor.

'That will be enough of that, Miss Webster,' said the man standing with Christina's mother. 'Please ensure that she does not hurt herself, Sergeant.'

'Sergeant?' said Christina, as the man next to her stepped forward, towering over her ominously. 'Mother? Who are these men?'

'They are policemen,' said Mrs Webster, her body shaking, her face chalk white, her fingers clenching themselves repetitively into fists. 'Christina,' she said, her voice dry and rasping. 'What have you done? What in heaven's name have you done? These men came to tell me such awful things and now . . . now your dear sister Agnes is . . .'

'Me?' said Christina. 'Nothing, Mama. It was the photograph. It was evil and I have destroyed it.'

'What photograph?' asked her mother, edging

towards her down the stairs. 'What are you talking about?'

'The photograph!' said Christina, getting angry. Her mother could be so infuriating sometimes. 'The one you brought back from that stupid auction. In a way all this is *your* fault, Mother. If you had not been so . . .'

'But I never bought a photograph,' she said. 'I bought a mirror.'

Christina looked at her mother in utter confusion and then down at the floor, at the dozens of jagged pieces of glass reflecting back at her. There was no photograph. There had never been a photograph.

She took this fact in just as the men came forward and grabbed her, holding her wrists and making her drop the gilt frame to the floor. As they led her away she began to remember.

It had been her that had sent the note to the police about Eva not having the correct papers to stay in the country. She had overheard her mother and Eva talking about it.

She remembered, too, how she had secretly visited her grandmother, getting in by the garden door, and persuaded the old woman to show her something in her bedroom, only to push her down the stairs and sneak out before any of the servants realised she had even been there – or so she had thought. But a neighbour had seen her and called the police.

She remembered holding the pillow down on Agnes's face and how her hands had searched blindly for Christina's arms and clutched at them, trying to pull them off, until finally they had grown limp and fallen lifeless at her sides.

Christina did not hang for her crimes as she might have done. It was decided that she was not of a sufficiently sound mind to be labelled a murderess. Her mother's inheritance was put to good use providing the best care at the very best asylum, and Christina's last wish was granted. She had a room of her own for the rest of her life.

Uncle Montague leaned forward, the firelight dancing in his eyes, smiling rather inappropriately considering the grimness of the tale he had just finished.

I looked across to the gilt frame hanging on the wall. If my uncle truly did believe that this frame was haunted in some way – that this frame was really the frame in the story and that story was true – then why on earth would he choose to have it on the wall of his study? I told myself that it spoke more of the irrational state of my uncle's mind than it did of the object, and yet once I turned away from the gilt frame, I had no desire to look again.

I licked my lips, my mouth feeling strangely dry, and my uncle offered me another cup of tea, which I gratefully accepted. All this tea, though, had its inevitable effect, and I excused myself in order to pay a visit to the lavatory.

In truth, I was never very keen on leaving my uncle's study alone and so put off such visits until I was on the point of doing myself some sort of mischief and almost had to run down the dark corridor to what my uncle always called the 'water closet'.

Uncle Montague gave me a light to guide my way, of course, but though this banished some of the darkness ahead of me, I was all too aware of the awful blackness behind me.

And locked inside the cramped lavatory I did not feel any more secure. There was a hole under the washbasin that I always found unsettling, having always had the foolish impression that something was peeping out and then retracting back into the shadows when I glanced down. A large web perpetually occupied a corner of the ceiling, though I never saw its maker.

As soon as I was done and my hands washed as well as they could be in the coffee-coloured water that ran from my uncle's taps, I moved to unbolt the door – I always ensured the bolt was fully home – and make the return journey with as much urgency as the outward bound one.

But just as I was about to pull back the bolt, the door handle was given a vigorous rattle from the outside. The noise and sudden movement of the handle startled me to such a degree that I almost fell backwards on to the lavatory seat.

'Hello?' I said. 'Uncle?'

Again the door handle was given a shake and the door was pulled with such strength I feared the bolt would not hold.

'Franz?' I said. 'I shall only be a moment.'

A long period of silence followed where I pressed my ear to the door and tried to detect any activity outside. I could not rightly say what disturbed me more – the rattling at the door, or the fact that it seemed so disembodied. What I did know was that I could not stay in the lavatory for ever.

I slid the bolt and opened the door. Peeping

nervously out, I looked one way up the long corridor and then the other. For as far as I *could* see – which was not far – there was nothing *to* see. I stepped out and began at once to march off in the direction of my uncle's study.

As ridiculous as it may sound, I was invariably seized with a strange dread of losing my way in that house. This sense of foreboding was heightened by the fact that I would be pursued by the mournful noise that came from the house's ancient plumbing when the chain was pulled on the huge and grotesquely ornate cistern. I was followed along the hallway by a noise that sounded as though a large animal had been caught in some kind of steam-driven machinery.

The enormous shadow I cast seemed to be racing me, trying to overtake me as I sped along, and a scuttling sound – which may have been Franz, though I never did look round to see – echoed around the corridor, as if something were running up and down the walls. I burst rather dramatically back into my uncle's study, panting with relief.

'Is everything all right?' asked Uncle Montague.

'Yes, Uncle,' I said. 'Of course. That is, there did seem to be someone trying the door of the lavatory.'

'Was there now?' said my uncle, staring off at the study door and frowning. 'Did you see anyone, Edgar?'

'No, sir,' I said. 'I expect it was Franz.'

Uncle Montague nodded.

'It could have been.'

'After all, sir,' I added, 'you said we were alone in the house.'

'Did I?' Uncle Montague murmured.

I put the lamp on the small table by the door and was about to join my uncle by the fire when I noticed something I had not seen before: a framed pen and ink drawing of some foreign landscape.

It was the kind of drawing that pulls you in to look at it and my uncle joined me in my examination of its skilful cross-hatching.

'Ah,' said my uncle. 'That is an Arthur Weybridge.'

The name meant nothing to me, but I raised my eyebrows and tried to look impressed.

'Where is it a picture of?' I asked.

'A small village in south-eastern Turkey. Have you been to Turkey, Edgar?'

'No, Uncle,' I said. I had been nowhere but to school and back, and though my uncle should have known this by now, I rather liked the way he always asked.

'Well, you must,' he said. 'You really must. Does your father have no interest in travel?'

'He likes to go fishing in Scotland,' I said after a moment's thought. 'But he never takes me. He says I would get bored.'

'And he is probably correct,' said Uncle Montague with a half-smile.

'Do you still travel, sir?' I asked.

Uncle Montague shook his head.

'No, Edgar,' he said. 'I used to, once upon a time. But now I must stay here.'

It seemed an odd thing to say – that he *must* stay in that house. My uncle had always struck me as a man of some means and I could think of nothing that should prevent his leaving. But then I wondered if he was referring to a medical condition I was unaware of. It might certainly explain much of his curious behaviour. I began to wonder if it had been he who had rattled the lavatory door handle.

'Are you quite well, Uncle?' I asked.

To my enormous surprise, after an initial silence he burst into a sustained bout of laughter. I could not think why what I had said caused my uncle such unrestrained amusement and it only confirmed my suspicion that his mind was troubled.

'You think me deranged, do you not, Edgar?' he

said, taking me by surprise by his apparent access to my thoughts.

'No, Uncle,' I said a little unconvincingly. 'You are tired perhaps?'

Uncle Montague grimaced.

'Yes, Edgar,' he said almost under his breath. 'I am very tired indeed.'

'Should I go and fetch Franz?' I suggested, moving towards the door.

'No!' said Uncle Montague forcefully, grabbing my arm. 'Franz does not like . . . visitors.' He let go of my arm and I was lost as to what I should do for the best. Uncle Montague looked at me and sighed.

'My apologies, Edgar,' he said with a weak smile. 'I did not mean to startle you. Perhaps if we sat awhile by the fire?'

'Of course, Uncle,' I said, and we both walked to our respective chairs.

We sat there in silence, the fire gasping and hissing, the clock ticking. My uncle began to drum the ends of his long fingers together rhythmically and I stifled a yawn.

'Since we are here, Edgar,' he said suddenly, making me jump, 'I could tell you about the drawing.'

'The drawing on the wall? Very well, Uncle,' I

said. 'If it would not exhaust you.'

Uncle Montague sank back into the shadows.

'No, Edgar,' he said. 'Thank you. I would rather be occupied. If you are willing to listen, then I am willing to tell the tale.'

JINN

Francis Weybridge was bored. His father, Arthur Weybridge, found this boredom intensely annoying, but being a mild-mannered Englishman, he expressed his annoyance by humming a little tune to himself and tapping his shoes on the gravel beneath their table.

The Weybridges, father and son, were seated in the tea garden beside the sacred carp pools in the town of Urfa in south-eastern Turkey in the twilight days of the Ottoman Empire. The sun had already disappeared over the nearby minarets and swallows were gathering to roost among the branches of the surrounding trees, squabbling noisily over their perches.

'I fail to see how anyone could be bored,' said Mr Weybridge. 'You are at the city once known as Edessa, the birthplace of Abraham, a place mentioned in both the Bible and the Qur'an. Look about you,' said Mr Weybridge with a theatrical flourish. 'Do you really mean to tell me that you find this dull?'

Francis made no reply but closed his eyes and sighed deeply, causing his father to hum once again, but this time a little faster. When Francis opened his eyes he saw a cat stealing up the tree beside them, disappearing behind the trunk and reappearing ten feet above their heads in the crook between two branches.

'So far on this journey,' said Mr Weybridge, 'you have been privileged enough to see Istanbul – the fabled Constantinople, jewel of Byzantium. You have stood beneath the great dome of Haghia Sophia. You have sailed along the Black Sea to Trebizond. You have travelled in the footsteps of Alexander the Great. Was it all "boring"?'

'Not *all*,' said Francis.

'Well, then,' said his father. 'I'm pleased to hear that, at least.'

It had not *all* been boring. Near Van he had seen a shepherd with a huge dog that wore a terrifying spiked collar. His father had told him it was probably to protect it from wolves. But this had been a small reward for such a tedious trip.

Francis looked up again. The cat edged along the branch above their heads. Now Francis could see the reason for the frantic jostling for position of the roosting swallows: none of them wanted to be at the end near the tree trunk. The cat lunged forward, grabbed a swallow in its teeth and scurried down the tree with its prize.

'This land is extraordinary, Francis,' said his father, lighting one of the noxious Turkish cigarettes he had developed a taste for. 'Wave after wave of civilisations have washed across its surface, and yet there is still something primeval about it.

'Jews, Christians and Muslims have all lived here and left their mark, but there is always the pull of something older, darker, more mysterious. Do you know there were pagans in Harran until the twelfth century?'

Francis had learned that any answer resulted in a lecture, so he kept quiet. Harran was a town nearby they had visited the week before. It was full of beehive-shaped houses and was mentioned in the

Bible. Francis had sat in the shade, watching his father draw while children buzzed about them asking for sweets.

It was here that Arthur Weybridge had been told of a village that was just as ancient and just as picturesque, but that no one ever went to. They would be visiting the village tomorrow, and Francis was not keen.

His father paid for their drinks and they walked back to the hotel. They ate well and Arthur Weybridge drank two gin and tonics, as was his custom, after which he began to tell Francis a long anecdote about his journey through the Russian steppes. It involved a Cossack and a three-legged dog and Arthur had already told it in Erzerum.

'I'm tired, Father,' said Francis, rising to his feet. 'I think I'll turn in.'

'Good idea,' said his father, downing the rest of his gin. 'We have a tiring day ahead. Goodnight then, Francis.'

'Goodnight, Father.'

They left in the morning after a breakfast of bread, honey and olives, the hotel manager's brother-in-law, Mehmet, driving them out of Urfa at bone-jarring speed in a rather ornate black carriage

Mehmet told them he had won from a Frenchman two years earlier in a game of backgammon.

The village was on a track branching off from the main desert road to Syria. Francis's father had intended to draw the traditional houses and the nearby Roman ruins, but as they arrived they saw policemen standing around.

Mehmet told them to stay in the carriage and went to find out what was happening. Moments later he returned with a man who introduced himself as the chief of police and told them that there had been a terrible accident: a boy had been attacked by a wild animal – a wild dog probably – and had been tragically killed. He could not be responsible for their safety while the beast was at large. He respectfully advised Mr Weybridge to draw somewhere else.

As Mehmet turned the carriage round, Francis saw the body under a blanket, a bloody hand exposed. He had seen, too, the looks on the faces of the children standing among the houses and wondered what secrets they were hiding. It was clear to him they were hiding something.

In fact, Francis had the distinct impression that even the chief of police was lying to them. He distinctly heard a boy nearby say 'gin'. Maybe the boy was not killed by animals at all but by a drunken father and they were trying to cover it up. But murder or wild animal, it was a lot more interesting to Francis than minarets and Roman temples.

'Father,' said Francis as they sat that evening in the hotel tea garden. 'Can we go back to that village? The one where the boy was killed.'

'Well, the police chief told us not to,' said Mr Weybridge. 'You have to be careful with these chaps, Francis. Why?'

'It just seemed interesting,' said Francis. 'I mean, there was just something about it. I can't say what. It seemed special somehow.'

Mr Weybridge smiled. At last! At last, Francis seemed to have been moved by something. 'I'll see what I can do,' he said.

The next day Mehmet reluctantly drove them back to the village. He had been talkative and irrepress- ibly jovial on their previous trip, but today he was sullen and tense. He had only agreed to take them at all because Arthur had paid him three times what he had the last time before they set off.

Mehmet clucked and flicked the reins, bringing the carriage into the shade of an old barn and the Weybridges got out. Francis followed his father about the village until he found the right spot for his drawing and opened up his camping stool and began to unpack his bag, taking out a wooden pencil box, a bottle of Indian ink, a pen and a sketchbook.

Francis had never been interested in his father's work, and now, after these past weeks, he felt something beyond boredom, something trance-like in which he would sit and let his eyes go out of focus and drift away into blankness.

Francis instantly regretted requesting that they return. Without the body, this village was even more dull than Harran. He was so sick of trailing round this godforsaken country. He felt as though he were being punished, and it all went back to 'the incident'. *Everything* had been different since then.

'The incident', as his father always referred to it, happened at school. A boy called Harris had taken a dislike to Francis and, over the course of a few months, name-calling and baiting had turned to casual blows and sustained beatings.

Instead of receiving the sympathy he had expected from his father, Mr Weybridge told his son that this was all part and parcel of school life and he would never be a man if he did not stand up for himself. He must deal with it. That was life.

So, one Sunday, after chapel, Francis waited for Harris with a cricket stump as he was walking past the tennis courts and attacked him without warning.

Francis had almost not gone through with it, having a terror that Harris would simply take the weapon from him and give him a thrashing with it, but Francis was overjoyed to find that his very first blow seemed to have knocked Harris senseless.

Laughing triumphantly, Francis leaped on the prone figure of Harris, raining down blows on his face and head. On and on he struck, his arm growing tired with the effort, until he was pulled off by a prefect who had heard the sickening thuds and run to Harris's assistance.

Francis's father was called and drove to the school that very afternoon. Francis found his interview with the headmaster, who ranted and slapped the desk so hard his lamp fell to the floor, far more preferable than his interview with his own father, who was quiet, even by his standards, and at his most annoyingly philosophical.

The fact that there were witnesses to testify that Harris had bullied Francis obviously counted for something, but Francis was annoyed to find that everyone seemed far more concerned with the fact that stupid Harris had almost lost the sight in his right eye than with the matter of his bullying. As far as Francis was concerned, he was a hero. Harris was a bully and he had done the school a service.

Most annoying was the attitude of Francis's father, who, having told his son to stand up to Harris, now sided with the teachers, who said that whatever the provocation this was not the behaviour they expected from their students. It was not what an Englishman did, apparently.

If Arthur Weybridge had not been as illustrious an old boy as he was, and such a generous benefactor to his old school, Francis would have been hustled out of school there and then. He was as unpopular with the staff as he was with his peers, but Francis would get another chance. It would be Harris who would go to another school, not he. There was some degree of satisfaction in that.

As it was, it was decided that the best thing for everyone would be if Francis was to leave school for a while and let things calm down a little. Mr Weybridge had been planning a trip to the Ottoman Empire for some time and so resolved to take his son out of school to accompany him. The trip would be an education in itself.

Arthur Weybridge was a bestselling author and

illustrator of travel books. He toured the world in his trademark pale linen suit and Panama hat, writing about the places of interest he passed through and crafting his famously dense and meticulous pen and ink drawings as he went.

For his part, Mr Weybridge hoped that his example of industry, enquiry and perseverance might rub off on his wayward son, who, though clearly intelligent, seemed to lack any interests at all. But two months into their journey, this hope was proving a forlorn one.

As his father began to become absorbed in his drawing, Francis's attention was caught by a group of children standing nearby. They were gazing warily off at something that Francis could not see, there being a house blocking his view.

Whatever it was, it was clearly frightening, because Francis could see fear in the faces of some, and a defiant if unconvincing show of fearlessness on the faces of others. He was intrigued to know the source of this unease.

He edged his way round the building until he left its shadow and recoiled, wincing from the sunlight's sudden glare. As he squinted he saw a strange shimmering figure up ahead, expanding and contracting like a reflection in troubled water.

He blinked and when he looked again there was a small girl, about eight years old, thin and hungry looking, dressed in rags. Her face was pale and expressionless, her hair lank.

Francis watched as one of the children picked up a stone and threw it at the girl. By skill or luck, the stone flew with impressive accuracy and struck the girl on the side of the head, above her right ear. Francis smiled and shook his head.

The girl hissed with pain and put her hand to the wound. Francis could see the glistening of blood even from this distance. He stared, fascinated.

Francis invariably watched the activities of those around him with the bored detachment of an audience at a rather dull theatrical performance. He could not have recalled with any certainty if he had ever actually cared about anyone in his whole life, and yet, to his enormous surprise, Francis felt himself taking an interest in this complete stranger. 'Why don't you just back off, you idiot?' he whispered to himself. But the girl stood her ground. Several children dropped to their haunches, looking for stones.

The boy at the head of the gang shouted at the girl, waving at her, pointing at her, shooing her. An idea formed in Francis's head that he could help

her. He could be a hero – a real hero. The notion amused him.

Francis walked towards the group of children as they began to take aim with their stones. He had expected them to scatter as he approached, but they seemed far less intimidated by him than they were by the girl.

'Leave her alone,' said Francis as he approached.

They looked blankly at him and Francis looked away to the girl and smiled in an effort to comfort her. When he looked back at the children, the boy who seemed to lead them was holding a large knife and jabbing the air between them. The ferocity of this small boy fascinated him. Francis cocked his head, peering at him, then he turned his back on the boy and began to walk towards the girl, who, infuriatingly, began to run as he approached her.

Francis chased the girl out into the flat rubble-strewn desert. Each time he was about to catch up with her, she put on another burst of speed, until he started to become annoyed. The sun hammered down mercilessly and Francis's eyes were stinging with salty sweat.

'I'm not going to hurt you,' he said, gasping, taken aback by the pleading tone of his own voice. 'I want to help you.'

As he strained to put one last breathless effort into catching her, he stood on a stone, stumbled, twisting his ankle painfully, and came to a panting halt. The girl stopped too. She turned and looked at him from under her heavy eyebrows. A voice sounded behind Francis and he turned round.

A long way off, standing between them and the village, was the gang of children who had been attacking the girl. Their leader was shouting at Francis and waving at him, shouting words he did not understand, though he could tell they were not complimentary.

There was something ridiculous about this little boy, made even smaller by perspective, goading Francis and beckoning him to come back. Francis smiled and limped over towards the girl, who now made no effort to run away. The children began to stoop down and pick up stones. Francis could see the sunlight glint on the boy's knife, but he felt no fear.

'You needn't be afraid,' he said. 'They won't hurt you while I'm here.' For the first time, the girl's expression seemed to lighten as her frown dissolved and she looked up. Francis basked in the glow of his good deed.

*　　*　　*

Arthur Weybridge had stopped drawing and, wondering where Francis was, had strolled through the village, up on to a small hill that shelved away sharply towards the desert.

What a magical place it was. The faint sound of children shouting was all that disturbed the tranquillity and he was struck by the contrast with how things had seemed when they had first come here. The memory of that attempted visit came back with sudden clarity – not just the commotion over the unfortunate death, but the remarkable fact that he had distinctly heard someone in the crowd utter the word '*jinn*'. Did these people really believe in genies? Then something caught his eye and, squinting into the blazing sunlight, he was shocked to see Francis some way off. He was not alone.

Arthur Weybridge tried to shield his eyes from the sun's glare. What on earth was Francis doing out there? Did he not realise how hot it was? And just exactly who or what was that with him? Why could he not focus on them? And what were those children shouting and waving about so hysterically? A strange dread began to come over Arthur. The word *jinn* flashed unbidden into his mind once more.

When he had first heard the word, it had

summoned up an *Arabian Nights* image of a genie in a bottle. But Arthur knew there were other *jinn*; there were evil *jinn*: there were the faithless *shaitan*, the shape-shifting *ghul* – ghoul, as we have come to call it – haunter of graveyards and barren places.

Arthur's eyes widened in horror and he began to run. The group of children were screaming as he passed them. One had a knife. He ran on, desperately trying to reach his son, shouting his name over and over.

Francis heard his father's calls but chose to ignore them. Whatever it was would have to wait. There was something about this urchin girl that intrigued him. People were seldom of any interest whatsoever to Francis, and yet this girl was different in some way.

Francis looked down and smiled at her and she smiled back: a wide smile, her lips parting, her mouth filled with shining white teeth. But they were the small, sharp teeth of a lizard.

Francis's body was lying on its back when Arthur reached it, one arm over his face as if to defend himself, a dark and cruel redness shimmering horribly at his throat. The thing that Arthur had chased away had dissolved into the heat haze: one moment animal, the next a girl, the next a woman, then an animal once more; then nothing at all.

Mr Weybridge stooped down and picked his son up and staggered back towards the village, humming gently to himself as he walked. The children who stood nearby parted to let him through, their heads bowed.

I took a deep breath, realising that I must have been holding my breath for some time and stood up a little more abruptly than I had intended. I walked back to where the drawing was hanging by the door.

'So this must be . . .' I began.

'Yes,' said my uncle. 'That is the drawing Arthur was doing when Francis went to meet his fate. It was the last drawing Arthur ever did, actually. He blamed himself for Francis's death and punished himself by depriving himself of his only real pleasure in life.'

'How sad,' I said.

'Indeed,' said Uncle Montague.

As I looked back at the drawing I noticed something. Standing in the shadow of one of the buildings was a figure – a small figure dressed in rags.

I was about to call my uncle to point out this discovery, when a curious thing happened. The figure seemed to shimmer as if the ink were still wet and then ooze into the rest of the drawing.

I blinked, amazed at this illusion of the firelight, or my overheated imagination, or both, and stared long and hard, trying to tempt the drawing to change again, but of course it did not and I returned to my chair by the fire.

'Did you see her?' said my uncle, gazing into the flames.

'Who?' I said, looking back at the drawing.

'Never mind,' said Uncle Montague. 'More tea?'

'Thank you, Uncle,' I said, returning to my chair. 'When you said –'

'Have you no desire to travel, Edgar?' interrupted Uncle Montague.

'Of course, sir,' I answered. 'I should like to travel very much.' Though the truth of it was, any desire I had previously entertained about visiting the land of the Turks had entirely evaporated. Just at that moment there was a noise above our heads, a noise that sounded like footsteps running from one corner of the room to the other.

I stared at the ceiling and Uncle Montague slowly did likewise. The sound of footsteps gave way to a shuffling, sliding sound, which seemed to centre on a rather large crack in the plaster.

'That noise, Uncle?' I said, still staring at the ceiling.

'It is an old house, Edgar,' he said, looking into the fire. 'It is full of noises.'

'But surely there is someone up there, Uncle?' I said. 'Are you not curious to know who it is?'

'No,' said Uncle Montague. 'No, I am not. I know who it is.'

I assumed by this comment that my uncle meant it was Franz, as of course it must have been. What is more, I had the distinct impression he was eavesdropping on our conversation. I even wondered if he could see us through that wide black crack in the plaster. My uncle seemed unconcerned and did not turn away from the fireplace.

'I wonder what he is doing up there,' I mused.

Uncle Montague nodded in a thoughtful way. He seemed lost in looking at something on the mantelpiece. I followed his gaze and saw a small photograph. My uncle noticed my interest and handed the photograph to me.

I was surprised to find that it was a wedding

photograph. It seemed rather sentimental for my uncle, and certainly out of keeping with the rest of the objects in the room. Perhaps it would provide me with some insight into my uncle's state of mind.

Looking closer I saw that the wedding couple was a rather unpleasant-looking man with huge side whiskers and a deathly pale woman who seemed too ill to stand, and who sat smiling weakly. There was a strange smudge nearby – some sort of stain on the photograph. I looked back at my uncle.

'Weddings, Edgar,' he said. 'They are grisly affairs, are they not?'

I had to agree, having suffered some interminable examples myself, during which I was forced to talk for hours to dreary aunts and uncles.

'Give me a funeral over a wedding any day,' said Uncle Montague with a sigh. 'The conversation is almost always superior.'

'Are they relatives, sir?' I asked.

'Not of mine,' he said. 'Or yours for that matter.'

'Friends perhaps, sir?' I ventured.

Uncle Montague shook his head.

'No, Edgar. I do not keep the photograph for sentimental reasons, I'm afraid, if that is what you were hoping. GO AWAY!'

I recoiled as if from a gunshot. There was a

confusion of scuffling noises on the ceiling followed by retreating footsteps. The echoing of the
old house gave the illusion of several pairs of feet
running away at great speed. Once I had recovered
from the shock I smiled to myself at the thought of
Franz's panic.

'You may not be surprised to hear that there is a
story attached to the photograph, Edgar.'

'May I hear it, sir?' I asked.

'Of course, dear boy,' he said. 'Of course.'

A Ghost Story

Victoria Harcourt stood on the lawn, spread out like the green baize of a billiard table. She was the unenthusiastic guest at a wedding between distant cousins. It was a sultry August day, the air thick and heavy like an invisible eiderdown. The lake beyond the lawn was still and dark.

The service had been a dreadful bore and the reception was no improvement. Victoria's parents inhabited the less wealthy branches of the Harcourt family tree and were always keen to mix with their more affluent relatives. Victoria stood self-consciously in her tired, unfashionable clothes and hated every second.

The wedding guests milled about beside a marquee while their children inhabited the garden. Her mother gave her encouraging nods in the direction of the other girls – cousins she had encountered all too often at similar events.

Victoria sighed and stomped towards the huddle of girls, all dressed in white and looking like a spray of carnations. An older cousin she particularly loathed, called Emily, was at the centre of the group, speaking in intense hushed tones. Victoria craned forward to hear.

'You know this place is haunted?' she whispered. The smaller girls in the group gazed open-eyed and looked to their older sisters for comfort. Emily let the effect of her words spread through the group and then continued.

'A famous murderer lived here,' she said. 'They hanged him and everything.'

'Gosh, Em,' said one of the girls. 'Is that true?'

'Of course it's true,' hissed Emily. 'Are you calling me a liar, Annabel?'

'No, Em, I . . .'

'Well, then,' she continued. 'It is true. You ask anybody. Bartholomew Garnet, his name was. He was evil, they say – pure evil. They hanged him at

Newgate in London. Papa told me all about it.'

'And the house is really haunted?' asked one of the smaller girls tremulously.

Emily nodded. 'As true as I'm standing here.'

'Have you seen the ghost, Em?'

'No,' she said. 'But lots of people –'

Suddenly there was flash of lightning, followed by a crack of thunder. The storyteller nearly jumped off the ground in panic and Victoria giggled. Emily glared at her. Rain began to fall in big, lazy drops, and then in a torrent that sent the ladies shrieking into the marquee, holding on to their hats.

'I say,' said Emily, recovering her demeanour and exchanging a sly look with her sister. 'Let's play hide-and-seek in the house.' Emily's sister grinned.

'But what about the ghost?' asked one of the girls.

'That will just make it all the more exciting!' said Emily. 'We'll play in teams of two,' she added bossily. 'Come on, Liz,' she said to her sister. 'We'll be "it". We'll count to a hundred in the library.'

The girls ran giggling for the house, leaving Victoria alone. She had seen Emily wink and knew they had done it on purpose to get away from her. If there was one thing worse than having to play with her dreadful cousins, it was those same cousins refusing to let her play. Victoria looked away towards the lake, the rain pelting the surface.

She was about to trudge back to her mother, when she noticed a thin girl a little younger than herself who had likewise been left behind. She was dressed even more drably and unfashionably than Victoria.

Victoria smiled. In those few short seconds, rain had already soaked the girl's clothes and was running down her face, dripping from her nose and chin. The girl smiled back and shook the water from her hair. Victoria would never normally have even considered talking to such a creature, but on this occasion she thought she might be useful.

'We ought to get out of the rain,' said Victoria.

'Rain?' said the girl, as if she had not noticed before.

Victoria laughed.

'Yes, rain,' she said. 'You're soaked.' Victoria realised she too was getting drenched as the downpour increased in intensity. She ran into the house and stood in the hallway. The girl followed, leaving drips and puddled footprints.

'What's your name?' said Victoria, wiping her face with her hands.

'Margaret,' said the girl.

'I'm Victoria. I suppose we're cousins,' said Victoria. 'Everybody here seems to be my cousin.'

'Yes,' said the girl.

'You're nothing to do with Emily, are you?' asked Victoria, peering at her. Margaret shook her head.

'Good,' said Victoria. 'I hate her. She is such a . . . such a . . .' Victoria could not find a word sufficient for her feelings. 'I hate her.' Margaret smiled and nodded. 'Let's be a team and play hide-and-seek,' said Victoria suddenly. Emily and her sister could be heard counting in the distance. They were already up to seventy-four.

'I'd like that,' said Margaret.

'Come on,' said Victoria, making for the stairs. 'Let's hide upstairs. There's bound to be somewhere up there.'

The two girls ran upstairs. Victoria had never been in this house before, but she had been in many like it. They all seemed horribly familiar in their scale and décor – all so much bigger and grander than her own house.

The first two places Victoria tried to hide were both taken and she was shoved and hissed away. She stood in the corridor, looking right and left, not knowing where to go next, when Margaret suggested they go to the door at the end.

When Victoria opened the door, she realised that it must be the master bedroom and wondered if they ought not to go somewhere else. But they could hear Emily and Elizabeth on the stairs, shouting, 'Coming, ready or not!' and Margaret had found the perfect hiding place: a huge blanket chest by the window.

Victoria lifted the lid and smiled when she saw it was empty. Margaret climbed in, and Victoria climbed in after her, closing the lid behind them as Emily came clumping down the corridor and found two of the cousins who had hidden behind the curtains near the landing.

The chest was huge. There was ample room for the two girls to sit, though they did have to bow forward a little awkwardly. Victoria's neck was already beginning to ache, but she was buoyed by the thought that she might get one up on the awful Emily.

'They'll never find us here,' whispered Victoria.

'No,' said Margaret and giggled.

'Shhh,' said Victoria, but then she giggled herself. 'Emily talks such rot,' she said eventually. 'I bet she's never been here before in her life. She always has to pretend she knows something about everything. Did you see the look on her face when the lightning flashed?' She giggled again. 'I wish he really was wandering about the house – that murderer who was supposed to live here . . .'

'Don't say that,' said Margaret.

'Oh come now, silly,' said Victoria. 'Emily was just trying to frighten everyone.'

Victoria found that if she craned forward a little she could just see through the keyhole of the chest, but there was nothing to see but the side of the bed. She could feel Margaret's wet dress against her leg and shivered.

Victoria listened to the muffled comings and goings of children on the other side of the bedroom door, as Emily and her sister hunted through the house. The rumble of footsteps would every now and then be interrupted by shouts and shrieks and girlish laughter as another pair of cousins was discovered. And each time Victoria and Margaret giggled, certain that they would be the last to be found. But as time went by, Victoria began to wish that someone would come in and open the chest. It was very dull in there with this girl she barely knew, though she was thoroughly determined not to give herself up.

It was uncomfortable. It was stuffy and musty

and surprisingly cold. Margaret's clothes had not dried out at all, and everywhere that Victoria touched seemed to be wet. She was sure she could feel water seeping through her dress.

Victoria put her eye to the keyhole again and gasped as something suddenly passed by, blocking her view. She instinctively pulled back. Her heart skipped a beat as she remembered Emily's ghost story, but the view quickly cleared to reveal white dresses and petticoats. It was Emily and the other girls, climbing on to the bed.

'Shut the door, Susanna,' hissed Emily. 'We'll get shot if we're found in here.'

'So come on, Emily,' said one of the girls. 'You promised to tell us the rest of the story.'

Victoria was filled with rage, clenching her fists until her fingernails sank into her palms. They had never been looking for her at all. Emily and the others had assumed Victoria would not get a partner and would simply go back to her mother. How she hated them. How she *hated* them.

She was about to jump out of the chest there and then and give them a piece of her mind, when another option presented itself. She would let Emily tell her ghost story, and when her audience was good and scared she would leap out and give them the shock of their lives. It did mean she would have to listen to Emily's tedious tale, but it would be worth it. She would have to hope that Margaret could keep quiet.

'So tell us about the murderer, Em,' said one of the girls.

'Well,' said Emily, settling back against the head-board. 'He was called Bartholomew Garnet, as I said. He wasn't a relative or anything.' There was a collective sigh of relief. 'He married into the family for money.' The girls tutted and murmured.

Victoria sneered inside the chest. How she hated these stuck-up little princesses. She could not wait to see their faces when she jumped out.

Emily, meanwhile, went on to tell the cousins how Garnet was a doctor, but not a very successful or wealthy one, who hadn't got a penny of his own. The woman who married him – a distant relative of Emily's father, called Charlotte – was his patient.

'She was a widow, very plain, Papa says, and was much older than he was. She was flattered by all the attention she was getting from the young Dr Garnet.

'She was already ill when they met – he was treating her. He was devoted to her and used to come at all hours of the day and night if she called. Everyone thought him a saint and any suspicions they had that his interest was solely in her money were extinguished over time. They married at Charlotte's insistence and she died not long after.'

'Murdered!' said one of the girls excitedly.

'Actually,' said Emily, 'she really was ill.'

'But I don't understand,' said Annabel, who was sat at the end of the bed. 'You said he was a murderer. You said he was hanged. Not much of a scary story, Emily.'

Victoria stifled a chortle inside the chest. Emily was such a terrible storyteller. This must be the least frightening ghost story she had ever heard. She was tempted to jump up there and then but she would give Emily one more chance to explain how this pathetic-sounding doctor came to be hanged and haunting the house.

'I haven't finished yet,' said Emily crossly. 'He was hanged all right. And I've seen a photograph of him I'll have you know, and if you'd seen his face, you wouldn't be so smug. He had awful, cold, piercing eyes. Even in a newspaper picture you could see how horrid he was.'

'Maybe he was wrongly hanged, horrid eyes notwithstanding,' said another girl.

'He was not wrongly hanged,' said Emily in an exasperated voice.

Garnet had confessed to murder, Emily told them. He was tried and convicted and, apparently, when he was hanged outside Newgate prison he appeared to look into the crowd and turn his face away, screwing up his eyes and begging the hangman to get on with the job. Witnesses said it was as if he saw his victim standing in front of him.

'Shhhh!' said Annabel. 'What was that?'

The girls became instantly silent and their eyes were wide open like startled deer. Victoria held her breath inside the blanket chest; she felt sure they could all hear her beating heart. But it was not Victoria whom Annabel had heard.

The sound of slow and heavy footprints could be heard in the corridor outside the bedroom door. They were some way off, but were coming closer. The girls stared at the door handle. The footsteps came to a halt. A floorboard creaked plaintively.

'I don't like it,' wailed one of the younger girls. 'Make it stop.'

Instantly the footsteps sounded again – faster this time and louder as they approached the door. Again there was a horrible silence. Then the handle rattled and the girls shrieked as the door creaked open.

'What on earth?' said the slightly flustered

middle-aged man who appeared in the doorway. 'I'm not sure you should be in here, you know.'

'Sorry, Uncle Giles,' said Emily, recovering her wits and smiling coyly. 'We just talking, sir. We will leave if you want.' Uncle Giles smiled, embarrassed by the attention of so many females.

'I'm sure you are doing no harm, ladies,' he said knowingly, and tapped the side of his nose. 'You carry on. Adieu, my lovelies.'

Uncle Giles fingered his moustache rakishly and left with a bow. Emily made a vomiting face and everyone did their best to stifle their giggles. They all began to settle themselves down once more.

'Where was I?' said Emily.

'You were saying that old what's-his-name was really guilty and really hanged –' began Annabel.

One of the girls interrupted to suggest that perhaps if Garnet *had* been wrongly hanged, that was probably why he haunted the house, because she had heard that ghosts are always annoyed about something. Another girl agreed, saying that her mother went to spiritualist meetings in London and had told her that ghosts were unhappy spirits.

'What are you *talking* about?' said Emily finally. 'I never said *Garnet* was the ghost.'

All the listeners, including Victoria, gave Emily a

puzzled look.

'If not him, then who?' Annabel asked.

'His victim, silly,' answered Emily with a sigh.

'But you said Charlotte really was ill – so did he kill her or didn't he?'

'Well,' said Emily with another sigh, 'if you would just let me finish, for goodness' sake. The ghost wasn't Garnet, or his wife.'

Emily went on to explain to her puzzled listeners that the victim was an orphan girl the kindly Charlotte had taken in from a local orphanage. Charlotte could not have children herself and doted on the girl. She was even going to be a bridesmaid at the wedding.

Charlotte already had a bad heart, but it was the mysterious disappearance of this girl that sent her into the illness that killed her. She and Garnet married as planned, but after Charlotte's death, when he had finally inherited all her money, Garnet turned himself in to the Justice of the Peace, admitting everything.

'But why did he kill the girl?' asked Annabel.

'It turns out that the girl saw the good doctor with the governess, canoodling in the shrubbery,' said Emily.

'Canoodling?' said one of the smaller girls.

'Kissing and cuddling,' said Emily, hugging herself and puckering her lips obscenely. The girls rolled around, giggling.

Emily went on to explain that the doctor had been pretending his love for Charlotte just to get her money all along. He sent the governess away, promising they would be together after Charlotte died. But Charlotte's adopted daughter threatened to tell her mother what she had seen. Garnet panicked and killed her.

He got away with the murder completely. The girl was wayward and unruly and everyone but Charlotte thought she had simply run away. Garnet helped to encourage the impression by stealing some jewellery and trinkets to make it appear as though the girl were a thief as well as an ingrate.

'What a beast!' said Emily's sister. Victoria shifted uneasily inside the chest. Her skirts and petticoats were uncomfortably wet now and she had become less sure about jumping out in that state, for fear that the effect would be more amusing than frightening. Perhaps she would wait until they had gone.

'Why did he own up?' said one of the girls.

'He said the girl started to haunt him,' said Emily quietly. 'She would appear suddenly, staring at him accusingly. In the end his mind snapped and he handed himself in.'

'How did he kill her?'

'He smothered her and hid her in a blanket chest until he could carry her out and dump her in the lake. They found her body tied to a big boulder by a rope. They say she wanders the house to this day, water still dripping from her clothes . . .'

Victoria burst from the chest like a crazed jack-in-the-box. As she had hoped, the girls in the room were suitably terrified. Two of them needed smelling salts to bring them out of a faint and one of them required laudanum to calm her when she came round.

It took two servants to restrain Victoria while another was sent to fetch her parents. She was screaming continually, only stopping when her voice would no longer function, huddled in a ball by the bed, staring at the empty chest.

I looked down at the photograph once more and saw this time that the smudge was no fault or fingerprint, but the blurred image of a young girl in a white dress; and the expression on the man I now knew was Garnet, which I had taken for arrogance, was actually more like the expression of someone holding their hand over a candle flame.

It really did look as if Garnet could see Margaret while no one else could, although something about his expression suggested that he was desperately trying to pretend that she was not there.

'The fog seems finally to be lifting,' said Uncle Montague, who was now standing by the window. 'You really ought to think about leaving, Edgar, while it is still light.'

I had been growing a little concerned about the approaching dark myself. It had only been my resistance to walking home in the fog – and my concern for my uncle's well-being – that had kept me so long. Besides, I was starting to feel as though I myself might become unhealthily influenced by my uncle's mental state were I to stay.

'Yes, Uncle,' I said, getting to my feet. 'Perhaps I should be getting along. I do not wish to worry Mother.' I winced a little at this transparent lie. My mother would barely have noticed my absence.

'Of course, Edgar. I am flattered that you would listen to the ramblings of an old man for quite so long.'

'Not at all, sir; I have been fascinated to hear your stories,' I said. 'And I shall look forward to coming back and hearing more.'

I stood a little self-consciously. I was of an age when I was still unsure of myself in such formal matters as greetings and partings. I had decided that I would shake my uncle's hand, but it didn't feel correct to do so while he was still seated and he showed no signs of getting up. Instead Uncle Montague smiled and picked up an old brass telescope that had been standing on the table next to his chair. Holding it to his eye he looked out of the window towards the woods. The smile seemed to disappear from his face as if he had seen some scene of great sadness to him.

'Uncle?' I enquired.

'It's nothing,' he said rather unconvincingly.

'I could not help noticing the telescope, sir,' I said. 'It looks like something a ship's captain might use.' Uncle Montague looked at the telescope in his hand but made no response. He merely looked back towards the woods.

'Uncle?' I said again.

'Forgive me, Edgar,' he said. 'I should not detain you. I have taken up enough of your time.' Still he did not stand, and once again looked down at the telescope.

'Does the telescope have a story?' I asked.

'Everything has a story.' Uncle Montague sighed. 'Everything and everyone. But, yes,' he said, cradling the telescope in his hands. 'This does have a particular tale to tell. But it can wait for another time.'

I looked down at my uncle, who seemed suddenly older, and I had not the heart to leave him.

'Please tell me, sir,' I said, sitting back down.

Uncle Montague smiled again.

'You may not thank me for telling you, Edgar.'

'Even so,' I said. 'Please tell me. One last story, Uncle, and then I shall away home.'

'If you insist, Edgar,' he said solemnly, returning to his seat by the fire. 'If you insist.'

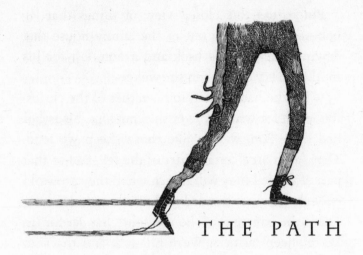

THE PATH

Matthew Harter came to a halt beside the huge lichen-encrusted stone that stood beside the entrance to the sheepfold and turned to take one last look at his home.

He almost changed his mind there and then as he looked at the huddle of stone buildings that had been the only world he had known for his short life, save for the fells and lakes that surrounded them. Matthew had lived all his years in that wild and mountainous area of the north country they call Cumbria, his family's house sitting at the base of the hills that girded it around like fortress walls.

But it was this closed view of things that lay behind his creeping out of the family house that dawn, a pack on his back and a note left for his mother to cry over when she woke.

When he had spoken to his father of the curiosity he felt for what lay over the crag tops, his father had said, 'Son, we are like those sheep we tend. They lamb on a certain part of the fell, and to that part of the fell they will return when they grow old enough. They are bonded to the hills and so are we. That's the course that the Almighty has set for us. We're sheep farmers. We're hill folk and that's an end to it.'

And so it was for Matthew's father, but not for Matthew. He had looked to his grandfather on his mother's side for another point of view; for though his grandfather, like his mother, had been born in the very next valley, he had escaped. He had run away to sea.

Matthew's grandfather had returned to the Lakes stuffed full of stories and needed no encouragement to tell them. He was a fine storyteller and even finer when his tongue was oiled with whisky. He was an institution at the Old White Lion until his death in the lambing season that year.

The only death Matthew had experienced prior

to that was of his favourite sheepdog, and it hit him
hard. It was as if a safety rope attaching him to the
outside world had been severed. With his grandfather's death, a whole world of possibilities seemed
to die.

This was not to say that Matthew was particularly fond of the old man, or the old man of him.
Matthew was only interested in the vistas his
grandfather opened up to him.

When Matthew sobbed through the funeral service at the little granite and slate church high among
the fells, the tears were for the loss of the stories,
not the loss of the man. If anything, Matthew felt
anger and resentment rather than sadness.

The tears were enough to convince his mother
that though the boy had not seemed especially
attached to her father, Matthew had obviously been
terribly hurt by his death. A few days after the
funeral she approached Matthew with a small
parcel, which when unwrapped revealed a brass
telescope.

'Father wanted you to have it,' said his mother.

'He did?' said Matthew, intrigued to hear a lie on
his mother's lips.

'Yes . . .' she said hesitantly. 'He thought you
might like it. It went all over the world with him

you know.'

Matthew held the telescope to his eye and was amazed to see the bracken beneath Brock Crag waving gently in the breeze as if it were only feet away, rather than the hundreds of yards away it actually was. His mother smiled at him and left him alone. It was at that instant Matthew decided to leave.

The telescope was a sign: a sign that he needed to get out of the valley and see the world for himself. He would walk to Penrith and take a stagecoach to Liverpool, and there he would sign himself aboard the first vessel that would take him; slave ship or whaler, he did not care, so long as it took him away from the place he was born.

He would need a little money, but that was all right – he knew where his father kept his cash and though, strictly speaking, it was theft, his parents would have one less mouth to feed. It was a fair exchange.

He might have picked up a ride in a cart had he walked the valley road, but Matthew had decided that that was not the way to leave somehow. He needed to walk the fell-top route to Penrith. He wanted his last view of home to be from above – to see it way below as he so often had in the past when he was up among the sheep on the high crags.

It was a fine morning but it was bitterly cold. There was a little snow on the high fells but not enough to put him off. He loved the fells best of all when they were white at their peaks like sugared buns, and it would be a fond memory for him to enjoy when he was basking in the heat of the Caribbean or the coast of Africa.

The sun was just coming up over the pass and the lake was beginning to glow like polished pewter. Birds were singing in the copse beside his house and among the twisted willows along the brook. Matthew took one last look at his home and walked away.

He crossed the road at the bridge and walked past the weavers' cottages. An old man who had known Matthew since he was a baby came to the door as he was passing, and Matthew felt suddenly guilt-stricken. He had an urge to go straight home, tear up the note and return the money he had taken. But his choice had been made. He must go on.

'Morning, Matthew,' said the old man.

'Morning, Mr Beckett.'

'Where you bound for at such an hour?'

'I lost something up top,' said Matthew. 'My grandfather's telescope. I was hoping to find it before my mother finds out.'

'Aye?' said the old man with a tone of scepticism that Matthew did not like. Who was he to question where a person did and did not walk? 'Well, I wish you luck then, young Mattie. He was a great fellow your grandfather. You must miss him.'

'Of course I do,' said Matthew more defensively than he had intended. 'I must be getting on. Goodbye, Mr Beckett.'

'Aye,' said the old man with a nod. 'You sure everything's all right, son?'

But Matthew was already walking away, heading towards the main path that snaked up towards the tarn and to the high drover's track that led to town. As he got to a sharp bend in the path, above the rows of the weavers' cottages, he took a smaller track – a barely perceptible sheep track – that ran by a massive stone barn and up the side of the fell, under the crags, rejoining the main path at the Black Tarn.

This was his path. He had walked it since he was old enough to walk anywhere without his brothers or parents, and though the track was clearly used by sheep and deer, he had never seen another person use it and felt it to be the only piece of this world that was his and his alone. There could really be no other route by which to leave it all behind.

He looked down at the weavers' cottages and smiled, imagining the conversation old Beckett and his father would have, but his smile quickly faded. He wished now that he had found the courage to tell the truth: that he was leaving this valley, these fells, this life; that he was following in his grandfather's footsteps and running away to sea. Unlike his grandfather, though, he would not be coming back.

He began to walk the narrow track, carefully tracing its path through the loose scree. It arced away up the fellside, its thin line so faintly impressed upon the landscape it was scarcely visible.

Matthew walked in the slow, evenly paced way of hill people. He could walk for hours with barely a pause for breath, keeping his feet to a rhythm that he dictated and not the ever-changing terrain. He was in no hurry.

A buzzard mewed as it quartered the hillside. Matthew could see smoke rising from the chimneys in the valley, but he would be on the tops before anyone realised he was gone. Even if they wanted to stop him, he would be beyond their reach.

The path grew steeper as it rose towards the crags

and Matthew regretted not bringing a staff with him. He was forced to scrabble up the last part as it squeezed itself through a cleft in the rocks, heaving himself up and over with his hands, the rock face icy to the touch.

Finally, he climbed up on to the crag and sat with his feet dangling over the edge, looking out over the valley. The sun was up over the pass now and sheep were bleating, calling to their lambs.

From where he sat he could see two lakes: one shining in the sunlight, the other, to the west, dark and brooding, grey from the reflected crags above it. Both were still as paintings, their surfaces like polished steel.

Matthew opened his pack and took out a hunk of bread and some ham he had taken from the pantry and ate it mechanically as if it were fuel and nothing more. The temperature suddenly dropped and the valley below darkened. He looked towards the east and saw clouds building, obscuring the sun. He pulled his collar up and held it close to his throat. He would be warm enough once he was on the move.

It was then that something caught his eye, way down below at the small outcrop of rock where the sheep track split off from the main path. Someone was following him! Matthew peered at the tiny form below him, frowning with incredulity and with an irritation born of possessiveness. This was his path, his alone!

It suddenly occurred to him that maybe his note had been spotted earlier than he had hoped and that this was one of his brothers sent to fetch him back. Even as he thought this, he knew it was not so. He had seen his brothers out on the hillsides a hundred times; he knew their shape and the way they carried themselves.

Besides, there was something strange about the way this figure moved, frantically clambering up the path. It was hard to see from that distance, but it almost seemed as though he – Matthew was sure that the person must be male – were running away from something.

Matthew could see that one of the stranger's arms hung at his side and flapped uselessly about like a rag doll's arm every time he scrabbled over a rock. The sight of it set Matthew's teeth on edge.

Worse still were the odd glimpses Matthew kept getting of the stranger's face. Mostly, the figure climbed with his head bowed, looking at the ground and Matthew could only see the top of his head, the hair seemingly wet and glinting dimly in the sunlight.

Occasionally, though, the stranger would look up, as if to check his route, and Matthew gained the impression that the fellow was wearing some sort of mask, or partial mask, as if he were a carnival figure. This, added to the stranger's bizarre movements, caused Matthew to shake his head in confusion.

He resolved to let the fellow catch up and pass him, deciding that the bother of having to exchange greetings with someone so odd was more palatable than having them dogging his footsteps. Then he remembered his grandfather's telescope.

Intrigued by the thought of getting a better look at the peculiar stranger below him, Matthew rummaged about in the bottom of his pack and took out the instrument. He put it to his eye and scanned the path, unable at first to find his target. He lowered it and when he had fixed the fellow's position, he put the telescope back to his eye and focused, the stranger disappearing momentarily behind a rock as he did so. As he reappeared and looked up towards Matthew, Matthew gave a cry and almost dropped the telescope over the edge. It was some time before he forced himself to look again.

The stranger was moving even faster than Matthew had imagined from a distance. He was indeed running and scrabbling upwards at a phenomenal rate. His motion was crazed and the eccentric movements of his body were now clearly explained.

His left arm was obviously broken – in more than one place, Matthew guessed. The left hand was scarcely recognisable as such, and looked as if a blacksmith had been hammering it. His left leg, too, was clearly smashed and flailed and juddered sickeningly as he moved. His clothes were ripped and sodden with blood.

The hair he had thought to be merely wet was clotted with gore and he looked as though he had been scalped by one of the American savages Matthew's grandfather had told him about. But it was the fellow's face that had caused Mathew to gasp in horror.

The features were utterly ruined and looked like something glimpsed in an abattoir or a nightmare. One side of the face was a hideous mass of gristle and torn flesh, like a sheep carcass after the rooks have worked it. An unblinking eye looked out from the other side.

Matthew immediately thought that the stranger

must have been the victim of some terrible assault – but by whom, or what? He had passed that way himself only half an hour earlier and had seen no one save old Mr Beckett. Besides, this fellow looked as though he had been mauled by a lion.

Why did he not cry out for help, thought Matthew, and how, when he was so badly injured, could he move like that? Matthew could not run up that track if the devil himself was behind him, and he was fully fit. He looked through the telescope once more, and once more he almost dropped it.

The stranger was not looking behind him as a terrified person might do, and neither was he looking up, as Matthew had previously thought, to check his path. As Matthew looked through the telescope the stranger looked up, not at the path, but at Matthew himself, and with an expression that managed to force itself through the ruined face – an expression of fanatical intent. He was not running *away* from someone. He was running *towards* Matthew.

Matthew scrabbled to his feet and stuffed the telescope into his pack. As he walked away from the crag's edge a scattering of snowflakes began to fall, but his thoughts were completely focused on the ghoul that was pursuing him. He had been on the fells in snow many times before. He knew these paths as well as anyone.

But within seconds the scattering of flakes had become a blizzard. He had never seen anything like it in his life. He had to narrow his eyes to slits to see at all; the view ahead was a blur of whirling snow.

The wind was so intense that he was forced on more than one occasion to turn his back on it and shield his face, and the wind seemed to be grabbing him and shaking him and trying to turn him about. Then he saw the shadowy image of the thing that was following him and he turned and ran.

He had some vague notion of trying to double back on himself and head for the path that might lead him back down to the safety of the valley and to his home. He would gladly take any punishment his father might hand out or suffer the scorn of his brothers, if only he might escape this hideous creature.

But as soon as Matthew began to run, he realised that he no longer had any idea in which direction the path lay, or in fact which direction anything lay. The snow was like a huge shroud winding about him until he could see no landmark at all, familiar or otherwise.

Still he ran, however blindly. The horror of the creature overtook any other fear he might have had. The snow stung his face, ice against burning flesh. Only once did he turn round, and there he saw the thing only yards behind him. He cried out weakly as a child might and then skidded to a halt, the toes of his boots hanging over the edge of a crag. As he turned, the ghoul walked slowly forward.

Matthew looked right and left, but there was no escape except through the creature that now loomed out of the swirling snow. Matthew began to sob and then yelled in despair.

'What are you? What do you want with me?'

The creature shuffled forward until he was only a foot or so from Matthew. The full horror of the injuries was now all too apparent, as was the fact that the clothes the creature wore were identical to Matthew's – so too was the pack that hung across his crippled shoulder. This realisation hit Matthew as he stared into the creature's one good eye, grey like his own.

'No!' he screamed, and the creature screamed with him, a cruel, distorted mirror of his own fear, and then Matthew fell, staggering backwards and plummeting from the crag on to the teeth of the scree below.

* * *

Mr Beckett was the first to find him. He was an old man and had fought as a soldier in his youth, though unlike Matthew's grandfather he never spoke of it; but still he had never seen the like of it. The boy's left arm and leg were smashed and lay at a sickeningly impossible angle to his torso – *and the face*...

Beckett only recognised Matthew by the clothes he was wearing. He turned away, his mouth dry and bitter with the taste of bile, threw his coat across the body without looking back and set off to tell Matthew's parents the grim news.

Uncle Montague smiled from the shadows at the look of horror I no doubt wore, and handed me the telescope. I almost had a mind to put it to my eye, but I was suddenly struck by a dread of what I might see – as if Matthew's horrible vision might still be clinging to the eyepiece. I grinned sheepishly at my own foolishness.

'Does something amuse you?' asked Uncle Montague.

'I was merely reminding myself, Uncle, that I am

getting too old to be so easily frightened by stories.'

'Really?' said Uncle Montague with a worrying degree of doubt in his voice. 'You think there is an age at which you might become immune to fear?'

'Well,' I said, a little concerned that I had once again offended his abilities as a storyteller. 'That is not to say that the stories you tell are not jolly frightening, Uncle.'

'Quite,' said Uncle Montague, though with a strange intonation.

'Have you ever thought of having them published, sir?'

'No, Edgar,' he said. 'That would not be appropriate. After all, they are not *my* stories, as I have intimated to you.'

'But I do not understand, Uncle,' I said. 'If they are not your stories, then whose are they?'

'They belong to those involved, Edgar,' he replied. 'I am merely the storyteller.'

'But how can that –'

'But I am afraid you really must go now, Edgar,' interrupted Uncle Montague, getting to his feet, his face suddenly serious. 'You would not like it here after dark.'

I failed to see what difference it would make as the house was in perpetual darkness anyway, but my uncle was already at the study door and as the fire seemed suddenly to have died away I was eager to follow him.

'Keep to the path, Edgar,' he said at the front door, with the touching concern he always showed me as I left his house. 'And do not tarry in the woods.'

'Thank you, Uncle . . .' I began, but the door was already shutting and I could hear a succession of bolts and locks being rammed home. I smiled to myself at my uncle's awkwardness at our parting. For such a worldly man, he could be charmingly shy at times.

But I did wonder if he had spent too many hours in his own company. His curious insistence that he was not the author of these tales struck me as most peculiar. It was obvious to one even as young I was then, that – as I had begun to explain to my uncle – in most cases, the principal characters in the story were dead by the end, or in such a tormented state that it would be hard to imagine how they would have the wit or the inclination to write or even dictate their tale.

But I did not think the worse of my uncle for this fabrication. I simply took it as a sign of his eccentricity. After a quick backwards glance at the house, I set off home.

I was never in any way tempted to stray from the path and, though I was sure that the woods were perfectly safe, nor was I inclined to dawdle. My uncle's concern was entirely misplaced. I would not have tarried in those woods for all the tea in China.

I had never before left it this late to return home and I was struck by how the darkness seemed to descend like a curtain, so that while it had seemed merely dusk when I left my uncle's door, night had truly enveloped me by the time I reached the wood.

As I did so I heard what I took to be my uncle's dog howling and resolved again to ask him about the animal, for I had never seen it in the grounds, nor had my uncle ever mentioned it. I was fond of animals.

Walking between the trees, I fancied that I saw shapes congealing out of the surrounding blackness and I became suddenly colder. I felt compelled to stop and peer into the dark to satisfy myself that I was troubled by my boyish imaginings and nothing more.

But quite the opposite effect was produced. Now that my eyes had become accustomed to the gloom, and now that I really concentrated my gaze, I could see that I was clearly *not alone*.

'Hello!' I called with a confidence I did not feel.

'Who's there?'

I saw by the silhouettes that the figures surrounding me were children. It was a group of the
village lads, rather a large group. As usual, they said
nothing – simply stood among the trees . . . silently
. . . malevolently.

I prepared myself for a beating; I could never
have reached the safety of my house before they
caught me. But I am English and have spent my life
at one of the finest schools in the country. I could
take a beating.

The crowd of boys moved closer. I could make
out none of their features as they seemed to bring
their own shadows with them. I tried to look as
contemptuous as possible, while steeling myself
against the punches and kicks I felt sure were about
to rain down on me.

But strange to say, instead of blows, tentative
fingers stretched out towards me, as if the children
– and I could now see by their silhouettes that
there were girls as well as boys in the gang – were
both afraid and eager to touch me.

'Enough!' said a voice behind me.

The children sprang back and I turned, startled,
to see my uncle carrying a lantern. I was relieved to
see him, of course, but I still had enough pride to

be a little embarrassed at being rescued by my elderly relative.

'Joseph, Matthew,' he said crossly. 'Leave him be.'

'You know these boys?' I asked, astonished that he knew their names and recognised them in such poor light.

'Yes, Edgar,' he said in a curious tone. 'I know these children well.'

'I don't understand, sir,' I said.

Uncle Edgar looked at me and smiled wearily.

'You asked me for one more story, Edgar,' he said. 'Very well, then. You shall have one more story: my own . . .'

Uncle Montague

'I was once a teacher, Edgar,' said Uncle Montague, stretching the muscles of his neck as if he was suddenly very tired. 'Did you know that?'

'No, sir,' I said. My uncle had never previously seen fit to tell me anything of consequence about his life.

Uncle Montague looked grim.

'Yes, Edgar,' he answered. There was an almost imperceptible movement among the surrounding children – as if they had all flinched at the same time. 'My house was a school then, and I was its headmaster: a cruel and wicked headmaster, Edgar.'

'Surely not, Uncle,' I said. The children seemed to have taken a step nearer, though they were still beyond the range of Uncle Montague's lantern.

'I am afraid so,' he said, casting a glance at the surrounding figures. 'I had begun my teaching life eager to impart the wonders of the world to my little flock of pupils, but over time, something happened to me, Edgar. I cannot say exactly what it was, but it was a kind of death; or rather something worse than death – a death of the soul.'

I moved to interrupt, but Uncle Montague continued.

'I wish that I could say my cruelty was of the ordinary sort – that I beat my children or forced them to stand for hours on a chair. I wish I could tell you that I humiliated them in front of their fellows. But no, Edgar – my cruelty was of a darker shade altogether.

'I wore the outward mask of a good and caring teacher, but unbeknown to those poor children, who looked up to me and worked so hard to win my praise, I was unworthy of their respect.'

Uncle Montague said these words with a heart-rending mixture of bitterness and regret and closed his eyes as if in prayer. The children around us bristled and inched closer. I gave a disapproving look to the child nearest to me.

'I do not understand, Uncle,' I said.

'I developed an addiction to games of chance, Edgar,' he said with a sigh. 'Finally settling on cards as my principal form of gambling. I was a good player, but even the greatest must lose, and lose I did. Gradually all my savings were eaten away and I was forced to look for another source of money to take to the table.'

'Uncle?' I asked, seeing the strange look that played across his face.

'I began to . . . *steal* from the boys, Edgar,' he said, looking away.

'Steal, sir?' I said, not quite able to take in the enormity of this crime – that a grown man, and a teacher at that, would *steal* from a child.

'You are right to be shocked, Edgar,' he said quietly. 'It was a terrible betrayal of trust. But it is one for which I have paid a very heavy price.' Again the children shifted noiselessly.

'I intercepted letters from the children,' my uncle continued, 'forging their handwriting and adding postscripts begging for money – money I intercepted as it came to the school. It did not stop at money. Presents sent to the boys by their doting mothers, I took for myself. I ate their birthday treats in my office and amused myself by offering the odd morsel to the boy for whom it had been intended. I had become utterly wretched, Edgar, and wallowed in my wretchedness as a hog revels in its own filth.'

I found it hard to meet my uncle's eyes and only the dread of seeing the shadowy figures grouped ever more closely about us persuaded me to look him in the face.

'Of course, these thefts were bound to come to light,' he resumed. 'And sure enough, I began to receive complaints from parents, as well as from some of the braver boys. I put them off for as long as I could, but eventually I was forced to act. I could, even then, have simply owned up to my crime and taken the resulting disgrace. How attractive that disgrace seems now, Edgar. I would embrace it now like a long-lost brother. But I was far too weak and odious to confess.

'Instead, another course of action occurred to me. There was a boy at the school. His name was William Collins. He was an orphan. His fees were paid through a firm of lawyers in the City. He was not popular with the other boys, for he was aloof and awkward.

'The curious thing was that it was this very aloofness that, even in the depths of my wretchedness, endeared him to me. It had been years since I had felt anything other than loathing and contempt towards the children, but I liked William. He reminded me of myself at his age.' Uncle smiled at the memory.

'But what has William to do with the thefts, sir?' I asked.

His smile dissolved.

'I had decided that I would implicate one of the boys in the thefts, Edgar. For some perverse reason I decided that I would choose . . . William: the one boy I had any fellow feeling for. To this day I cannot say why.'

'And did it work?' I said, surprised by how cold my voice sounded.

'Yes,' said Uncle Montague grimly. 'The boys were only too ready to accept it. William came to me, pleading with me to make them understand that he was innocent. I reassured him that I would do everything in my power, but of course I did nothing at all.' Uncle Montague looked straight into my eyes, his face like a carved mask. 'He was badly beaten.

'Parents demanded that something be done about this thief. I wrote to William's lawyers, explaining the circumstances and requesting, with great regret, that they place William at another school.'

'And what happened to him, sir?' I asked.

Uncle Montague sighed. The children scurried forward a few inches.

'William came to my study. He was distraught. His face was bruised. He had been beaten again. I could not bear to see him in that state and know that I was the cause, but instead of standing up and putting an end to his misery, I sent him away. I told him that he must face these things and be a man.'

'And then?' I asked, fearing the answer. My uncle made no response. Every silhouetted face turned to his, and they seemed to be urging him silently to answer.

'What happened then?' I said again.

'He took his own life, Edgar.'

I gasped with horror.

'Yes! He took his own life, driven to it by my lies and vile trickery. No one knew my part in his death, but the suicide was enough to persuade parents to take their children away from the school and soon it was empty of all but the most unloved boys, and there were few signs of attracting new blood.

'William's death had shaken me, of course, but I had no idea of the journey I was yet to embark on.

Gambling was at the root of all my problems, but so addicted was I that instead of simply stopping, I decided to let chance decide my fate. I swore that if Fortune let me win, then I would dedicate myself to needy children hereabouts. If I lost, then I would give myself up to the authorities and answer for my past misdeeds.

'I found a whistle I used to wear around my neck in happier times. It was a whistle I used to rally the boys when we were engaged in one of our many nature trails or historical outings. I had not used it in many a year and I put it in my pocket as a lucky charm. Gamblers are as superstitious as sailors, Edgar.

'I decided I would take all the money I had squirrelled away to a rather dubious club in town and play the cards one last time.

'As I reached the door of the club and was about to climb the dimly lit steps to its entrance, I saw out of the corner of my eye a group of shabbily dressed children standing some way off in the shadows on the other side of the road. The presence of those urchins should have served as a reminder of my purpose as I entered the club, but I was already forgetting my oath.

'Much to my surprise, my luck had changed. I

could not lose. One by one, my fellow gamblers cashed in and left as the pot grew larger and larger. Other customers of the club came to watch. I had never won so much money in all my days of gambling. As I left the club, loaded with cash and promissory notes I looked for the children, but there was no sign of them. I took the whistle from my pocket and gave it a grateful kiss. I hailed a cab, spent the night in the Savoy and returned to the house the following day.

'My final night of gambling was nothing of the sort, of course. No gambler wins like that and stops. Instead, I spent some of my winnings on fine clothes and tried my luck at another, more salubrious club near Piccadilly.

'Once again, as I paid the cab and tapped the pavement with my silver-tipped cane, I saw a group of children standing some way off in the shadows. It seemed a strange coincidence, and I took their presence as a good sign.

'So it turned out to be. I won again and hand-somely. In fact, I won every time I went to the card tables. I won so often that I was accused of cheat-ing, but though I would not have been above such a thing, I just seemed to be having a run of the most extraordinary luck. The clubs began to refuse me entry, of course. They could not prove that I was cheating; it was enough that I was ruining their businesses.

'My gambling club days were over. So I invested some of my winnings and discovered that I had the same good fortune in my investments that I had enjoyed at the card table. I seemed unable to lose. I was soon rather rich and I must say I enjoyed it. I was now perfectly placed to pursue the course I had promised myself – to engage in an act of benevolence and educate the unfortunates of the local area. But I had not changed, Edgar.

'In fact, I closed the school and sent the few remaining children away. All thoughts of my promise to school the local children had left my mind. I returned the house to the grand residence it had been in former times and began to receive the attentions of a relative – a nephew who lived nearby, whose interest in me just happened to coincide with my new-found fortune.'

'My father?' I said.

'Your father?' said Uncle Montague. 'No – your grandfather, I think. It has been so long I cannot recall. I was never a family man.'

'But that would make you –' I began.

'Very old indeed,' said Uncle Montague. 'Yes. The

house keeps me alive, Edgar – after a fashion.' A strange expression played across his face. 'But I did not know that then. I was still in a state of blissful ignorance. I was so wealthy that I did not care. I could do what I liked now. Or so I thought.'

'What do you mean, sir?'

'One day, Edgar,' said Uncle Montague, 'I was standing in the grounds of my house – the gardens were quite lovely then – and realised that I still had my old school whistle in my pocket – my lucky charm from my gambling days. I felt a tiny pang of regret for breaking my promise, but it passed like a bout of indigestion. I took the whistle from my pocket and put it to my lips. I had a sudden urge to hear its cheerful trill once more.

'I blew, but no sound came. I told myself that the whistle was broken, but I came to realise that it was not broken but altered; it had become akin to one of those special whistles only dogs can hear. Though I heard no sound, I was aware of some vibration in the air that rippled outwards. The sky clouded over and the temperature dropped. I shuddered, and not only with the cold . . .'

'Uncle?' I said, for he seemed to have drifted into a kind of daze.

'Ah yes,' he said. 'That was when they began to

come: to come in answer to the whistle's silent call.'

'The children?' I asked, looking at the group gathered about us and wondering how it could be that they would hear a whistle my uncle could not and why they would come to its sound. I feared for my uncle's sanity more than ever.

'The children, yes,' said Uncle Montague. 'They are my punishment, Edgar.'

'Your punishment, sir?' I said, wondering what hold these local boys could possibly have over him, though he seemed at ease in their company and had no qualms in sharing the shocking details of his life with them.

'The house is an accursed place, Edgar,' he said. 'You must have felt it.'

'There is a strange atmosphere, sir,' I said. 'It is a little cold.'

Uncle Montague chuckled at this and I saw the children flinch.

'A little cold?' he repeated. 'Yes, Edgar. It is a little cold. Is that not right, children?' This was the first time he had addressed them and they became agitated, though they remained silent throughout.

'You have still not explained what these children are doing here, Uncle,' I said.

'Can you not guess, Edgar?' he asked.

'No, sir,' I said. 'I cannot. Are you educating the village children to make amends for what happened at your school?'

He smiled grimly and shook his head.

'These are not village children, Edgar. I think that in your heart you know that.'

'Sir?' I said, determined to cling to the rational. 'What do you mean?'

'They tell me their tales, Edgar,' he said. 'They come to me and tell me their tales. They bring me some token of their story and these accursed objects now litter my house – a house now utterly drenched in a strange otherness that contaminates the walls and grounds and the man you see before you. It is a magnet for creatures of a twilight world, Edgar, a world you cannot imagine. The house calls to them as lamplight calls to a moth.'

'But if the house is so awful, sir,' I said, doing everything in my power to avoid looking back towards the shadowy children. 'Why do you not leave?'

'Oh, Franz would not like that, Edgar,' he said. 'And it does not do to upset Franz.'

'But I do not understand, Uncle,' I said. 'Franz is your servant.'

'Franz used to be my servant long ago, when he

234

was fully alive . . .'

'When he was fully alive, Uncle?' I said. 'But what can you mean? Either someone is alive or he is . . .' I could not bring myself to finish the sentence. My uncle's guilt had clearly unhinged his mind.

'The house has changed Franz utterly,' he said. 'There is no way he would let me leave, Edgar, even if I had the will to try. He is more jailer than servant now. But it is no more than I deserve. There are many breaking rocks and rotting in stinking jails for far lesser crimes than I have committed.' He paused. 'But strange to say, Edgar, I no longer fear my visitors as I once did. I am at peace. I have accepted my fate. It is my punishment for those years of not listening to my pupils, for not listening to William.'

'You cannot mean to say, sir . . .' I began. 'You do not mean to say that the stories you tell me are from these children's lips?'

Uncle Montague nodded.

'But how can that be?' I asked, faltering slightly as the children craned forward, seemingly hanging on my every word. 'Surely that would mean . . .'

'Yes, Edgar?'

'Surely that would mean these children – some

of these children, at least – were . . . *dead*?'

At that word the figures all around us leaped away and disappeared into the trees, peering out from behind the trunks, and though they were beshadowed as before, I knew that every eye was trained on me.

'They do not like that word, Edgar,' said Uncle Montague. 'It disturbs them.'

'It disturbs *them*?' I said, only the fear of running headlong into one of these phantoms stopping me from fleeing that instant.

'They bring me their tales and I listen,' my uncle went on. 'William was the first, though I knew his tale all too well, of course. Ever since then, they have been coming to me. I am like a strange cousin of the Ancient Mariner, Edgar. Do you know the poem?'

The children were regrouping around us now.

'Yes, sir,' I said. 'Samuel Taylor Coleridge. We had to learn great pieces of it by heart last term.'

'I am doomed, not as he was to tell his own terrible tale, but to listen to the tales of these lost children. It is my punishment and my penance.'

One of the children now reached out a tentative hand towards me and, despite my sympathy for their suffering, I let out an involuntary whimper of fear.

'NO!' boomed my uncle in a terrifying voice that opened an unwanted window on to the figure he must have struck in his days as headmaster. I recoiled instinctively and the shadow children did likewise.

'He is not yours,' said my uncle. He turned to me again and his voice mellowed. 'Forgive them, Edgar. They are drawn to your beating heart, to your body's warmth. They have a terrible hunger for life. They mean no harm, but their touch . . . can chill to the bone. It is time you went home, Edgar.'

'Yes, Uncle,' I said, but still remained where I was, unable to turn my back on those spectral creatures.

'Come, children,' said Uncle Montague, gathering them about him as if they were setting off on a nature ramble. 'I don't suppose I shall be seeing you again, Edgar.'

'I do not know, sir,' I said.

'I would quite understand,' said Uncle Montague with a sad smile. 'Though I should miss your visits. It has been a comfort to me to have someone to share those tales with. Farewell, Edgar.'

With that he turned away, and the children followed him along the path. I watched, heart pounding, until the glow of his lantern became a firefly in the distance.

I realised now that the names he had spoken when he first appeared – Joseph and Matthew – were names of boys from the tales: Joseph, who had been the victim of the creature who guarded the elm tree, and Matthew, who had fallen to his death after being confronted by his own horribly disfigured self.

As I watched, one of the children turned and began to walk back towards me. I say 'walk', but it was a grim mockery of a walk – a strange lurching hobble. I knew who it was before my uncle spoke his name.

'Matthew!' he called reproachfully. 'Come along. Leave Edgar be, there's a good lad.'

The beshadowed spectre came to a halt a few yards from me and seemed to cock his head quizzically. He shuffled a little closer and I had a dread that I might see that terrible face, the face that had driven the living Matthew to his death.

'*Matthew!*' called my uncle again, more forcefully this time. Matthew turned and hobbled away. Air rushed back into my lungs and I realised I had been holding my breath.

Finally I gained the courage to turn and head homewards. Uncle Montague had put 'The Rime of the Ancient Mariner' in my head and a verse came

back to me as I hurried along, head bowed, hungry
for the dull normality of my parents and my home:

Like one, that on a lonesome road
Doth walk in fear and dread,
And having once turned round walks on,
And turns no more his head;
Because he knows, a frightful fiend
Doth close behind him tread.

Chris Priestley is the acclaimed author of the spine-tingling *Uncle Montague's Tales of Terror*, *Tales of Terror from the Black Ship* and *Tales of Terror from the Tunnel's Mouth*. His other books include *New World*, *The White Rider*, *Redwulf's Curse* and *Death and the Arrow*. Chris is also an illustrator, painter and cartoonist. He lives in Cambridge.

David Roberts is an award-winning illustrator who has worked with a huge variety of authors, including Philip Ardagh and Georgia Byng. He is the creator of the *Dirty Bertie* series. David lives in London.

For more information visit
www.TalesofTerror.co.uk